# THE PERFECT SPOUSE

A Novel by

# SIOUX DALLAS

CCB Publishing
British Columbia, Canada

The Perfect Spouse: A Novel

Copyright ©2009 by Sioux Dallas
ISBN-13   978-1-926585-62-8
First Edition

Library and Archives Canada Cataloguing in Publication

Dallas, Sioux, 1930-
The perfect spouse : a novel / written by Sioux Dallas.
ISBN 978-1-926585-62-8
I. Title.
PS3604.A439P47 2009   813'.6   C2009-906197-X

Disclaimer: This is a book of pure fiction, a product of the author's imagination, and does not represent any person, living or dead.

Extreme care has been taken to ensure that all information presented in this book is accurate and up to date at the time of publishing. Neither the author nor the publisher can be held responsible for any errors or omissions. Additionally, neither is any liability assumed for damages resulting from the use of the information contained herein.

Publisher:   CCB Publishing
British Columbia, Canada
www.ccbpublishing.com

*To Virginia Bryant, a true Christian friend who*
*not only talks the talk, but walks the walk.*
*Thank you is not enough.*

*They are known by the fruit they bear.*
*Matthew 7:16-18*

# ACKNOWLEDGEMENTS

There are friends too numerous to list who have been angels to visit, call, supply food, bring cheer-up gifts and pray, during my medical problems.

The ladies from my Bible study class, students from my Aqua Champions Aerobics and ladies from Cairo Court #97, Ladies' Oriental Shrine of North America have been true blessings.

From my Bible class Rosemary Adams has supplied several full meals. Our Bible teacher, Helen White has brought food and gifts. Mary Ann Austin has visited often and I have her prayers. From the aerobics Linda Snow and Rose Shaw have supplied full meals. Carol Glennie, Fran Silver, Ellen Leedy, Caroline Sklenar, Jean LaFevers, Carol Schneider and Claudia Weaver have supplied food and gifts. Linda Snow, Lisa Alicea and Rose Shaw have supplied frequent transportation. All of the others, men and women, have given of themselves. I love all of you, not for what you've done for me, but by being your own loving self.

Don't walk in front of me; I might not follow
Don't walk behind me; I might not lead
Walk beside me and be my friend

# MYTH

There is an old English saying that: when a baby gets ready to leave Heaven and be born on Earth, that its guardian angel placed a finger on the lips and says, "Shhhh. Don't tell what we say and do up here."

A cleft or indentation is left on the upper lip which is a blessing. The child, who has this, has more blessings than the one who doesn't.

# PROLOGUE

Although there was almost a foot of snow on the ground, and more promised, the sky was blue and clear. The air was nippy, but invigorating.

Only twenty-four days until Christmas. The street and stores were beautifully decorated and the gaiety of the people, walking on the streets, was infectious.

He thrust long, artistic fingers through brown, wavy hair and gave a sigh of indecision. Drawing his chin down into his overcoat against the bitter cold, he viewed the building he was facing. His sea-green eyes held a look of uncertainty gazing at this particular place of business. His brown Armani suit and overcoat were expensive but tasteful. A cream Stetson and snakeskin Western boots looked good on him. The white shirt and red tie completed the outfit. His boots were shiny, but, by the way he was walking in the slush, they wouldn't be for long.

Snow laying in heaps along the building fronts and in the gutters, had begun to turn to slush and was icy. There was little traffic. People were only in cars when they absolutely needed to go to work or important appointments.

His expression was thoughtful and slightly sad. Should he or shouldn't he? Should he enter this building and take a chance on someone accepting him just as he is, or should he walk on?

A year ago he had buried his beloved wife. They had only been married ten months when a home invasion left her beaten and dead. He had been at work and was inconsolable when he came home and found her.

Recently he had visited a friend who had an auto accident. At the friend's house, he had found a copy of The Blade newspaper from Village of Fayette, Ohio. The friend had lived there and extolled the virtue of the people and town so strongly that he decided to move here as he could not be happy where he and his wife had lived. He had left Lynchburg, Virginia and moved here to Fayette, Ohio and opened a CPA office.

This lovely town of Village of Fayette had less than fifteen hundred people and was only one and two tenths square miles. There were loads of larger cities and shopping malls close. There was one public school and one privately owned preschool.

There was emergency medical help but no big hospital in Fayette. There were eight or nine major hospitals close by. Five various religious organizations were in the town.

The village atmosphere was more of a rural community. Middle income families, single-family homes, apartments and condominiums provided housing. Industrial plants and business on Main Street provided employment. There were several fine dining opportunities.

He was pleased to find a Lions Club, of which he was a member and Normal Memorial Library where he looked forward to spending many pleasant hours. There was a Village Police Department with full-time chief, some officers and auxiliary officers. A township/village Fire Department with a part-time chief and thirty-five volunteer fire fighters were available with the Fulton County nine-one-one.

He had met the police Chief Aaron Mason and the Pastor of the Community Faith Church, Dr. Charles Black, during the first week he had lived here. His apartment was three blocks from his office and was a good, pleasant walking distance.

He had hired Grace Miller for a receptionist as soon as he opened the office three weeks ago. She came highly recommended and had been a secretary for an aged attorney, who had died and left her with no employment. During the first week he had been open, he hired Elizabeth Mitchell who had three and one half years of college and was determined to finish with a BA in Business Administration. Although she was engaged to be married, she stated that she expected to continue working.

During the second week, Gregory Martin had applied for a job stating that although he had graduate training, and came highly recommended, he was staying at home to care for his invalid mother. Greg had been hired and Jason felt he had an excellent staff.

Taking a deep breath, he reached for the glass door to The Perfect Spouse which was a dating agency. He wasn't interested in a permanent relationship, but wanted to find new friends in church and, hopefully, in here.

# CHAPTER ONE

"Hello. Welcome to The Perfect Spouse. Please have a seat. My name is Corella Swanson and I'm the manager. How may we help you?"

"I'm Jason," he said nervously, "Jason McBride." He sat cautiously in the comfortable leather captain's chair and looked around. He was in a large, open room with maroon carpeting and three long tables. Near the front was an arrangement of several small, round tables and chairs to offer a pleasant opportunity to visit with other people.

Corella flipped an ash-blonde page boy cut that framed a sweetheart-shaped face. Long eye lashes framed hazel eyes and fell on peaches and cream complexion that needed no cosmetics. Her five-four height appeared taller due to the three inch stiletto light green suede heels. The ridiculous heels complimented the A line lime-green sheath that flirted just below her knees on well-shaped legs. Gold fan-shaped earrings dangled from small ears. Dimples danced in and out on both cheeks.

"Well, Jason. We're very glad to meet you and hope you'll be interested in joining with us. We have forms for you to fill out which will tell us about you. Then we match you with a nice lady whose information will be compatible with yours."

"I -- I'm not so sure about this. I just want information."

"That's fine, Jason. There's no pressure on anyone. Everything is confidential except what you wish to share with others. Why don't you read through these papers and then decide what you want to do." She handed him several sheets of paper on a clipboard and two number two pencils.

Jason walked over to a round table of black and white swirled marble top.

Farther back there were three long tables and two desks with a lady at each desk. Doors showed rooms on two sides of the long room.

He sat in a comfortable, padded Spanish-style chair and read through all the papers. He then slowly, and carefully, began filling in the information.

There was a promise of confidentiality. The fee for joining would be thirty dollars and thirty dollars per month for membership. Anyone could resign at any time without penalties.

NAME: Jason Allen McBride
ADDRESS: 286 Main Street, Apartment 2B, Village of Fayette, Ohio, 43521
TELEPHONE: 419-555-8095 - home 419-808-7964 - office
DATE OF BIRTH: November 16, 1979
AGE NOW: 30
HEIGHT: 5'11"
WEIGHT: 187
HAIR: Brown
EYES: Hazel-green
NATIONALITY: Caucasian (Irish, Italian)
OCCUPATION: Accountant (CPA)
EDUCATION: BS in Business and Accounting, Masters in Business and Accounting. Minor in music

LIKES: People just because they're people, animals, especially horses, reading, walking, hiking, church and music.

DISLIKES: Eating in public alone, bitter cold, overly spicy foods.

I WOULD LIKE TO MEET SOMEONE: who is interested in being friends and take time to see what develops. I'd like someone who is not possessive, who enjoys musicals, attends church and who likes people.

TELL SOMETHING ABOUT YOUR CHILDHOOD: Here he hesitated. How much should, or could, he share? He wanted to forget the earlier part of his childhood. From the age of six he was raised, and loved dearly, by maternal grandparents. His beloved Grandpa died during his second year of college and his Grandma had died just as he graduated from college.

While in his third year he had met Linda Ann Preston. She was a type A personality and loved him for his shyness, gentleness and beautiful baritone voice. They attended the same church and both sang in the choir. During their last year he had proposed and was so pleased that his much loved Grandma had approved of Linda and was looking forward to their wedding.

Jason and Linda were married soon after graduation. He was only sad that his grandparents were not living to rejoice with him.

His Grandma had always said "The truth is best, even if it hurts. If you once tell a lie, you have to tell more to cover up, and soon you'll forget what you've said and get caught.

He finally wrote about his fond memories and how fortunate he was to have had so many wonderful people in his life. His beloved mother had died just before his fifth birthday and his father was killed in an accident when he was six. He didn't tell his father was in prison, killed during a fight.

# CHAPTER TWO

Rory Leigh McBride was a tall, big man, not fat, just muscular. He was a retired Marine Captain and was now a deacon in his church as well as a well decorated police investigator for the county. He had blondish brown hair and green eyes. Everyone was respectful and admired him. Rory's personality slowly changed so that he received several reprimands in his work which made him furious. He took it out on his family. People began to be suspicious, but none knew what really went on behind the doors at the McBride home.

Mary Margaret Pistolo McBride was a sweet, loving woman five-five, about one hundred ten with long, chestnut hair and hazel eyes. She was a passive person with a slight frame and a beautiful soprano voice. Rory was pleased that she often trembled in fear in his presence. She loved her little boy dearly, but left the room when Rory came in.

Rory was thrilled to have a son to brag about, but was angry when people stated that he looked like his mother. The baby was happy, loving and out-going. He loved music and to have stories read to him

The little boy was strikingly handsome with light brown hair and hazel-green eyes (mostly green) and a beautifully shaped mouth. There was a deep cleft on the upper bow-shaped lip and on his chin. People said he was too pretty to be a boy. He was always laughing, singing and loving people. He especially liked and enjoyed the children in his Sunday Bible class. He would sing all the way home and tell about the wonderful Bible stories. Rory was annoyed with the boy's exuberant nature and his happy chatter.

\* \* \* \* \*

One Sunday, when Jason was three, almost four, he rode happily home from church singing and talking as he always did. As they walked in the front door, Rory grabbed him by the back of his shirt screaming at him.

"You were very bad today. I looked through the window on the door and saw you and Troy Mitchum punching each other and laughing. You were not even listening to the lesson."

"But Daddy, I was listening. We were enjoying the story about the little boy who fought a giant and won because the little boy trusted God and asked for His help." (David and Goliath)

"Don't talk back to me. You'll remember this." Rory slapped Jason so hard on the back of his head that the little boy fell flat on his face. Rory put a foot on Jason's back, took off his belt, and proceeded to whip Jason.

The shocked little boy yelled and cried. Rory roared, "Stop that infernal noise. Don't yell like a baby or you'll get more licks. I'll teach you to be like a man." Jason tried to be quiet even though he hurt and his heart was breaking. He felt he must have done something awfully bad for daddy to treat him like this.

Rory finally stopped, picked Jason up by the back of his shirt and shoved him down the hall toward his room. "Get in your room and be quiet. You'll get no lunch."

Jason ran to his room as fast as his chubby little legs could take him. He wanted to slam the door but was afraid to. He fell on his bed and muffled his cries in a pillow.

Mary Margaret silently served her husband a delicious lunch of fried chicken, potato salad, deviled eggs, green beans with small onions and mushrooms, yeast rolls and Jason's favorite, banana pudding with a thick, nicely-browned meringue. She could not eat because her heart was breaking for her precious baby boy. Rory ate savagely, burped, didn't say anything to Mary Margaret as he got up from the table. He swaggered into the living room, plopped on the couch, turned on the television to a ball game and went to sleep.

Mary Margaret had grown up in a home where she was taught that the man of the house was the head, in control and no one questioned his decisions or actions. The difference was, her father had been a gentleman who loved and respected his family and was loving and kind. She was appalled at her husband's treatment of the little boy but did not speak out against him, after all, he was the head of the house.

After Mary Margaret had cleaned the dining room and kitchen, she tiptoed in to discover her husband asleep. She quietly hurried back to the kitchen. Her heart beat so strongly with fear of discovery that she was afraid it could be heard.

She placed a chicken leg, two tablespoons of potato salad, a deviled egg, a big spoon of green beans, a yeast roll on the plate and a glass of milk on a tray. In a smaller bowl, she placed a huge helping of banana pudding.

Jason heard his door softly opening and was afraid it was his father. He scrunched his eyes shut pretending to be asleep. When he felt a soft, sweet kiss on his cheek, he hurriedly sat up to hug his mother. His eyes were round with amazement at all the good food.

"Shhh. Be quiet. I want you to know you're my good little boy, and you've done nothing wrong. I don't know why daddy was so angry, but I bet he's sorry for what he did. Eat this and I'll sing to you. Then I want you to really take a nap."

Jason ate the oh, so good food with an eye on the banana pudding. He knew he could not eat it until he had cleaned his plate. His mother softly sang and hummed to him. He had one bite of the pudding left when his door flew open.

"Ah ha! I suspected as much. Now you'll get no dinner. Mary Margaret, come into our room. You and I need to have a talk."

She hugged Jason again. "I love you my little man and you **are** good." She tucked him under the sheet, walked quietly out and shut the door. Jason hid his head under his pillow so that he could not hear the cries of his mother.

# CHAPTER THREE

Jason awakened later to find the next door neighbor, Mrs. Irene Silver beside his bed.

"Well, hello darling. I'm going to stay with you until your grandparents get here. Your daddy took your mother to the hospital. She has a broken wrist and some minor injuries. She said she fell." Jason said nothing. He knew better, but wasn't sure what to tell.

Irene picked Jason up and carried him into the living room where her husband, Matthew, was sitting. They cuddled him between them and soon Grandpa Michael Pistoli and Grandma Terry Pistoli were there. The two couples visited for a few minutes and then Grandpa hurried home with Jason after Grandma had packed him a bag. Grandma stayed for a few days to help her daughter.

Jason never knew how angry his daddy was to find her there or how angry he was to find Jason gone. Three days later he called Grandpa and angrily demanded the return of his son.

Rory continued to hit Jason and make him afraid to move out of his room when daddy was home. Mary Margaret was taken to the hospital frequently with broken ribs, twice a broken arm, and other minor, but painful, injuries.

\* \* \* \* \*

Two weeks before his fifth birthday, Jason was devastated to learn of the death of his beloved mother. Rory had said she tripped, in the dark, over some concrete blocks in the back yard. She never regained conscientious and died two days later.

Dr. Albert Hammond had been suspicious concerning Mary Margaret's injuries, but could do nothing because she always told him she was careless.

The Medical Examiner, Dr. Lawrence Backes, was a friend of Dr. Hammond. The two men talked about this death and came to the agreement that proof of broken bones and damaged flesh showed physical abuse.

The maternal grandparents brought charges against Rory and gained custody of Jason. The medical reports, coupled with the reports of bad attitude at the police department, gave Judge Hiram Weaver grounds to conduct a trial, charging Rory with manslaughter. He was given fifteen years in prison, but during his second year was killed by another inmate during a fight.

\* \* \* \* \*

Jason always thought lovingly of his sweet mother, but loved and appreciated his grandparents. They encouraged him to get the best education possible, to sing as much as he wanted to and to have compassion for other people. He grew up loving Bible study and trying very hard to live as he should.

\* \* \* \* \*

Jason took the papers to Corella, reiterating that he wasn't sure what he might do in the future.

"Jason, there's no pressure on any one. Do you think you'd like to join and get acquainted? Then you could decide what you want to do permanently."

"I guess so --- for a few months."

"Good. Jenny," she called to a young woman at another desk. "Please come here. This is Jason McBride. Jason, this is Jenny Carson. She's our Treasurer and will take care of you."

"I shall be delighted to help Jason. Please come down here with me.

Okay, Jason, I'll need sixty dollars, but from now on it'll only be thirty dollars a month. How do you want to pay?"

"May I write a check? I make it a habit not to carry much money."

"Sure. We'll take your check." She took the check and gave him a receipt. "We want you to be happy and satisfied, Jason. Please let us know if we can do anything to help you. Now, I want you to meet Dottie Fingar. She's our membership chairman and will help you make a video and have a still shot."

"Hello, Jason. Welcome. I'm glad to meet you. If you'll come with me, we'll get a still shot first and then make a short video."

"If I make a video, why do I need a still shot?"

"The still shot goes in these book here on this table with a short paragraph about you. Ladies look through the book and if they like the picture, they'll ask to see the video. If they're interested, we'll notify you and you come in and look at their video. If you, too, are interested, we'll arrange a meeting here in the club and the two of you will go on from there."

"Will I be expected to contact any lady who asks to meet me?"

"Oh, no. That's up to you, and the same goes for the ladies. If they are not interested in further contact, they can just ignore the request."

"Thank you. May I call you Dottie?"

"That's my name," she laughed. "We're all first name here." She proceeded to take a shot of him and then led him into another room to make a video. "I'm going to leave you alone for a few minutes. Here's a pad and pen. If you wish, you can write what you want to say. It will keep you from getting nervous and giving a less than sterling impression."

Jason decided to just give his first name, his height, his hobbies and his likes and dislikes. It only took five minutes to make the video.

"Very good. Tomorrow your picture will be in the book and your video will be in our collection. You can check on your own efforts any time; keep the video as is or change it."

"Thank you, Dottie. I told Corella that I'm not sure about this, but I'm willing to give it a try."

"Great. We have a get-together, with refreshments, usually on the second Saturday of each month at seven P M. You'll meet the staff and members on that night."

"Am I required to attend?"

"No. Not every one attends or some come in once in a while. The owners try to promote a family style atmosphere. They would like everyone to be friends and encourage each other."

"Why the name, The Perfect Spouse?"

"Elaine Harper and Joseph Harper are the owners. She said she has been so happy in her marriage of forty some years, and feels she has a perfect spouse. She wanted others to find someone and be as happy as they are."

"Catchy name. Thank you for your help." He nodded to Dottie and lifted a hand toward Jenny and Corella as he left. He wanted to keep this to himself, for the time being. Not to be secretive, but he felt shy about joining a dating agency when there were several nice ladies in the church. Too, he wasn't sure how long he would continue to be a member.

Walking off, Jason did not know that Corella had already called Chief Mason and asked him to check his data base and see if a Jason McBride had an undesirable record. The owners of The Perfect Spouse tried to be very careful as to whom they let in and introduced to other people.

# CHAPTER FOUR

Jason's clientele grew so rapidly they were all busy Monday through half day Saturday. Jason was grateful for the confidence shown in him by the people in town and in surrounding areas.

He was so busy that he shoved his joining the dating agency into the back of his mind. He was jolted four days later when Grace called him to say there was a Dottie Fingar on the line, but she didn't know what she wanted. Jason thanked her and waited until he saw her light go off to start talking to Dottie.

"Jason, we have a request from a lady to meet you. How soon can you get here to view her video?"

"This is most unexpected and my office is so busy." He hesitated.

"Maybe I can get there for a few minutes around two. Will that be all right?"

"Certainly. We're here for your convenience."

Nervous spasms hit Jason's stomach. *Will I like her picture? Will she like me in person? What can we talk about? Should I take flowers this first time?* He decided to wait and let nature take its course.

Jason stayed in the office and let the three go out for lunch. Grace brought him a Ruben, a latte and an apple pie. He ate quickly and donned his overcoat. Walking to the front he told Grace he was going out for a brief time on personal business. He placed a Stetson on his head as he walked out of the door.

\* \* \* \* \*

"Hello, Jason." Corella greeted him as he came in the door and removed his hat. "I think Dottie is waiting for you."

"Do I have to make a decision now?"

"No, Jason," she assured him. "You've paid good money to be a member and it's up to you what you want to do, or how often you want to meet ladies. If you'd rather wait until after your first get together and then decide, that'll be your privilege." Dottie walked to them.

"Let me think about it. Remember I told you how apprehensive I am."

Dottie laughed. "I'm familiar with the feeling. You're not the only one who has been unsure. Put your coat and hat on the rack over there and come with me."

He saw a polished copper rack with crooked arms reaching from it. The end of the arms had round copper balls to keep from damaging clothing. He placed his overcoat and hat on the rack and followed Dottie. She took him to the end of the long, open room where two thick books about fourteen inches by ten inches were on a table.

"The green book has the ladies pictures and the blue book has the gentlemen. Let me see." She read off a paper in her hand. "Oh, yes. The lady you want to check on is number 4352."

She opened the book for him and showed him the picture of a woman, possible in her early thirties. She had strawberry blonde hair, green eyes and a sweet smile. The name under the picture was, Rose, and she stated that she loved the outdoors and music. He read through and then

15

asked to see the video. Out of curiosity he looked for his own picture and smiled to see he was number 4896.

"May I see her video now?"

"You certainly may. Come with me to the video room."

They walked out into the hall and down two doors where they entered a room with comfortable padded chairs. There was a small table to the right of the door which held water, coffee, sugar, cream and swizzle sticks. There were also a variety of pastries, paper cups and napkins.

"Jason, if you wish, you may use these little pads and pen to make notes or write questions you might like to ask later. Would you care to get coffee and a Danish first?"

"No, thank you. I don't think my stomach would appreciate anything now because I'm nervous about this."

She smiled. "Don't feel badly. You're just experiencing what the majority of people feel when they start. It is a big step to take and we understand that. All of you are strangers to each other and there has been horrible publicity about other dating agencies. The owners, the Harpers, are extremely careful about whom they allow to participate. You probably were not aware of it, but everyone is checked out by our police chief. If the person has a questionable record, or suspiciously no record at all, that waves a red flag and they are not encouraged to continue."

"Really! Was I checked out? Now that was silly. Of course I was."

"I'm positive you were. But to ease your mind, the chief hasn't given any warning about you, so that means you're A okay. If you attend the party on Saturday week, you'll meet the owners, staff members and some of the agency members. Not everyone attends."

"But it isn't required to attend."

"Oh, no. Please consider it though because you'll meet new people and have a chance to get acquainted. You may even meet the lady who asked to see your video."

"Do we have to tell our names and about ourselves at these parties?"

"No. We go on first name only unless you wish to tell more.

"Do the staff personnel ever date the members?"

"No. It's against the rules. Now have a seat. Did you get your pen and paper? I have the video and will put it in the machine for you and you may view it as many times as you like. I'll leave you in here and will return in a few minutes. I hope you enjoy this experience." She walked quietly out.

"Hello. My name is Rose. I'm twenty-eight years old and single, meaning I've never been married. I've been too busy getting an education, working in a bank, caring for elderly, sick parents until their death, and keeping up with a few social obligations. My parents came to Maryland from Hungary in 1927. They proudly became citizens and taught my two older brothers, one older sister, me and one younger brother to take pride in our citizenship and be patriotic Americans."

"After they died, I left Maryland and journeyed to Indiana to take some classes at the DeVry University for a Business Degree. I have a Masters in Journalism and have been working for The Blade. I also have sold some news, and my own short stories, and doing freelance work to other papers in other cities. My roommate was from Fayette, so I decided to visit her home, fell in love with the place and people, and have been here for four years."

"I'm five-seven and I'm not telling my weight," she laughed. "Not that I'm overweight, but a girl needs to have a few secrets. As you can see, I'm a strawberry blonde and have hazel-green eyes. My eyes change color according to the color of clothing I'm wearing, although they're mostly green."

"My hobbies are reading, baking, golf, traveling and meeting people. I like people just because they're people, although I'm sometimes shy or hesitant about meeting new people. I do attend church but haven't joined one. I dislike too spicy foods, being out in cold weather, people who are often late and loud, rude people."

"I would like to meet someone who also likes and accepts people, who is not quick to judge, does not have a temper and likes music. I play a little piano and like to sing, but it's questionable whether other people like to hear me sing."

"I grew up in Maryland in a warm, loving family. My siblings and I keep in touch on a regular basis. My parents expected good behavior, good effort at whatever we were doing, good manners and to accept responsibility for our actions. I hope this tells you enough about me until you want to get better acquainted. Blessings."

Jason sighed and looked at the notes he had jotted down. Would he need to see the video a second time? He didn't think so, but still wasn't sure what he would do about contacting this lady. She seemed nice and had some of the same likes and dislikes that he had. While he was sitting and thinking, Dottie came back into the room.

"Do you need to view the video again or do you have any questions?"

"No, thank you. I think I'll just go home and ponder what I've seen and heard. I'm inclined to wait until the party to make any decisions."

"That's fine, Jason. We start at seven and dismiss at nine. Not everyone stays the full time. Some of our members come from nearby areas and we don't want to keep them on a winter night. In the spring, when the days are longer, and the time changes, people have a tendency to stay later."

"Thank you for helping me. I guess I'll wait for the party."

"That's your privilege. I'll see you out. I'm sure there'll be requests from other ladies to meet you. Why don't you take the time to look through the book of ladies and see if you'd be interested in asking to meet any of them?"

He hesitated. "I'd like to do that. They returned to the first room to look through the book out of curiosity. After he had looked through the book, he told everyone goodbye and thanked them for their assistance.

Jason said nothing to his staff about joining a dating agency. He was a little embarrassed about it and basically was a private person. Not so secretive, just private.

# CHAPTER FIVE

The time passed quickly and the Saturday rolled around for the party. Jason took a shower and laughed at himself for being nervous. He felt as if he was shaking visibly and he was perspiring heavily. He dressed carefully in new jeans in a western cut. The sage-colored turtle neck sweater complimented his eyes and coloring. He drew on white cotton socks and a pair of brown Western boots. He loved those boots.

He checked his wallet to make sure he had drivers license, insurance cards and some money in the event he wanted to go somewhere after the party. Slipping a watch with a stretchy bank on his left wrist, and a ring that belonged to his grandfather on his finger, he checked himself in a full-length mirror on the back of his bedroom door.

Taking a deep breath for courage, he slowly walked out and to a closet in the hall just before entering the living room. He took an overcoat and a Stetson out of the closet and whispered a quiet prayer.

*"Lord, I really don't know why I'm talking to you. I've had to endure so much heartache and cruelty that I've, at times, felt that you no longer cared about me. I've been taught better by my precious grandparents. They said You never leave us, that it's we who leave You. I'm trying very hard. If You're still with me, give me the wisdom to make the right decisions and help me to be the man my grandparents raised me to be."*

He left the apartment, locking the door behind him. He rode the elevator down to the underground garage and entered his two year old blue Camry. He carefully backed out and started on his journey. At that time of night it didn't matter where he parked as long as he wasn't blocking a fire hydrant. He had to sit in the car a few minutes and talk himself into going into The Perfect Spouse when he observed so many cars parked on the street and beside the building in a small lot.

Slowly climbing out of his car, and touching the button on the remote to lock it, he walked into the building. Bright lights were spilling out on the sidewalk and rousing music could be heard faintly. He opened the door and was hit with music, the cacophony of voices, laughter and the odor of fresh-baked pastries.

On one of the long tables, near the front, was a thirty-two cup coffee pot, a big pot of hot water and a basket of a variety of tea bags. There was regular sugar, artificial sugar, and cream beside four big trays of a variety of pastries. There were also finger sandwiches and a big bowl of cut fruits.

Napkins, paper plates, small paper bowls and swizzle sticks were in abundance.

The room was decorated with Christmas lights, good-smelling greenery and beautiful ornaments. In a corner was an eight feet tree beautifully decorated with gaily wrapped packages on a red velvet skirt under the tree.

He had noticed that in the window was a scene to represent old Jerusalem. There were handmade houses, an inn and an ice-cream stick stable with straw inside. The full nativity was in place including lighted angels and a star on top of the stable. Eye catching and interesting.

On a small table near the window was a menorah and items connected with Chanukkah. On another small table were items acknowledging Kwanzaa. Jason was impressed with the thoughtfulness of the religions.

"Jason. Hello. I'm glad you decided to join us. Leave your coat in the room over there," Amanda greeted him. "Come on with me and I'll introduce you to the staff and some of the members."

"No. Please. Can't I just blend in and look around?"

"Whatever you wish, but the Harpers will want to meet you."

"Who're they?"

"The owners. And the rest of the staff will want to meet you."

"Well, okay. Lead on McDuff," Jason grinned nervously.

"Would you like refreshments first or do you want to meet everyone first?"

"I'll have to meet the staff sometime, so I might as well do it now.

Amanda slipped her hand into the crook of his right arm and led him to a couple who reminded him of his grandparents. The man, about six feet tall had beautiful silver hair and sky blue eyes. His ruddy complexion showed he was an outdoor person. His muscles and rugged appearance led one to think he either worked out often in a gym or participated in a lot of outdoor exercises. He wore tan slacks and a yellow shirt with no tie. Jason guessed him to be early sixties.

The woman was about five-six, small build, obviously dyed black hair, and brown eyes. She wore a natural sweet, laughing expression and moved toward Jason as if she already knew him and was glad to see him. She was dressed in a long, green gown with white lace trim around the neck. Small silver heels with pointed toes peeped from under the gown. He guessed her to probably be sixty.

Amanda smiled and greeted the older woman. "Elaine, you'll enjoy knowing one of our new members, Jason."

"Jason, welcome, welcome, she gushed with an honest voice. We want to help you and make your life as happy as possible. If we can do anything to make your membership with us happier and worthwhile," she tittered, "don't hesitate to tell us how you feel." She turned and looked around. "Joe. Come here, please," she called to the tall man.

"Joe, this is Jason, one of our new members. I'm sure you'll want to get acquainted with him."

The man hurried to them with a wide grin and his hand held out. "Jason, that's a manly name. We're glad to have you in our family. Now that you're one of us, feel free to call on us for anything."

Jason hardly knew what to say. The couple seemed to be sincere, but he had learned to wait until he knew people before he made a decision. He smiled and thanked them.

Amanda smiled at them. "Excuse us. I'm going to introduce Jason to the staff." She turned him around and faced a crowd of people. "Now you've met the owner, Elaine and Joe Harper, I'll introduce you to the rest of the staff.

Jason was not really interested in meeting others, but he went with her although he only truly wanted to walk around and observe.

"Jason, you've met Corella Swanson, our manager. This is Anthony Petrillo, her assistant. Tony is responsible for organizing our parties."

The two men greeted each other. Jason noticed that Tony's smile didn't show in his eyes. Tony was about five-ten, about one sixty with close cropped black hair and brown eyes. His brown complexion showed a Mediterranean heritage. Jason guessed him to be early thirties. It was obvious Tony thought well of himself. He had on blue dress slacks with a sharp crease in them; a grey silk shirt and a blue and red stripped tie.

"You've met Dottie who is responsible for the membership records and you've met me. I'm her assistant. Jenny Carson is the Treasurer. This is Andrew Murray her assistant and in charge of publicity. He'll remind you if you ever forget to pay your dues."

Jason was cordial to all he met, but knew he'd have trouble keeping them in mind until he got better acquainted.

Andrew Murray, called Drew, attached himself to Jason and encouraged him to return to the refreshment table. "You'll meet a lot of people tonight and you'll have trouble keeping them separated. Don't let it bother you, Jason, just relax and enjoy the evening."

Jason looked down at Drew, guessing him to be five-eight and about one fifty. His dark brown hair was cut short and Jason smiled to himself thinking that Drew cut it short to keep the curls in control. He had beautiful grey eyes, a wide mouth that smiled a lot and a pleasant face.

Drew excused himself to welcome another new member which relieved Jason. He wandered around looking at the room and observing some of the people. He was startled when someone slapped him on the shoulder and boomed, "Hi there. My name is Gary Beaumont and I've been a member since the place opened. I've enjoyed dating some lovely women, but I'm not looking for a wife at the present. How about you?"

Gary was the same height as Jason, but not as heavy. In fact, he was very slender even though he looked healthy and quite able to take care of himself. His red sweater with white reindeer and snowflakes around the bottom was just right with his navy slacks. His light brown complexion led Jason to think Gary was African American, at least part because he had dark brown hair and amber eyes.

Jason had observed a mixed crowd, which was good. There was even a couple of Native American and one or two who looked Oriental. He looked at Gary not really wanting to socialize, but was too polite to ignore him. "My name is Jason and I just joined." They talked for a few minutes.

When Jason saw a couple of women heading in his direction, he excused himself, hurried into the room with the coats and outer wear, grabbed his overcoat and hurried out. He had had all he could take for this one night. No way did he intend to tell his full name and much about himself until he was better acquainted. He thankfully pulled into the underground garage and got out of the car.

"Hey, neighbor."

Jason whipped around to see an older couple exiting a car near him and beginning to walk toward him.

"Hello," he called. "Excuse me, but I have to hurry home."

He was almost breathless when he all but ran into his apartment and firmly shut his door and locked it. *Who was that couple? I don't remember seeing them before. Apparently they live here, but I don't know anyone in the building yet.*

Jason prepared for bed, set his alarm to get up earlier than usual and fell into bed, thankful to be in his own home. He had probably been asleep about an hour when he sat up startled at a loud banging on his door.

"Hey, buddy. Open up and let us in. It's party time. Don't be an old stick in the mud."

"Yeah, don't stick in the mud," another voice giggled as only a drunk could do.

Jason didn't recognize the voices and could not imagine who might be in a drunken state outside his door. He tiptoed into the living room and looked through the peep hole. Two very drunk strangers were staggering around yelling and laughing. He didn't know either man and did not open his door.

He was relieved when the door across the hall was jerked open and a man stepped out. He recognized him as the man who had spoken in the garage. The man was irate; after all it was eleven.

"What do you men want? Get away from here. There's no one here that knows you or wants you. You're waking people that need their sleep."

"Oh, yeah? Well, our buddy, Frank, knows us and he'll want to let us in and party with us." The man speaking began beating on Jason's door again and yelled. "Frank. Come on out and tell this jerk that we're going to paaarty, paaarty."

The man across the hall spoke up again. "There's no one here by that name. Frank does not live here. You're at the wrong apartment."

Apparently the woman had called the police because two officers showed up just then and arrested the two drunks. Jason waited until they were gone and then stepped out in the hall. The man was still standing there looking at the police leaving.

Jason looked at the man. "I'm sorry you were bothered, but I honestly did not know those men."

"Don't worry, son. I've seen enough of you to know you don't mix in company like that. My name is Tony Dixon and this is my wife, Betty." He turned to the woman who was standing in their doorway.

"I'm glad you're living across from me. I don't know that I would have done anything about those drunken men other than to ignore them. I'm glad to meet both of you," he smiled. "My name is Jason and I've got to get up early to go to work. If you'll excuse me I must get back to bed and hope I can sleep some. Thank you again."

"Oh, I've already made hot chocolate. Do please join us," Betty said with a smile.

Jason reasoned to himself that they were probably lonely and it wouldn't hurt him to have one cup of hot chocolate.

He grinned sheepishly and pointed to himself dressed in pajamas.

"You're fine," Tony urged him. "It won't take long to drink a cup of hot chocolate. We're in night clothes, too. Come on over for a few minutes."

Jason shrugged and walked over into a homey, pleasant room. Tony showed Jason to sit on a lovely old-fashioned tan camel back couch. He sat and found it surprisingly comfortable. Betty came in with a tray on which were three mugs of hot chocolate with marshmallow on top. Beaming, she handed mugs to the two men and then took one and sat down.

Tony raised his mug and said, "To good friendship."

Jason smiled, inclined his head and said, "Hear, hear."

Betty brought out pictures of family. Jason learned they had a daughter who had married an Arab and now lived in Iraq with grandchildren they had never seen. They had two sons, both killed in service. He could tell they were heartbroken. In reality they had lost all three of their children. Jason quickly realized that they were not only lonely but needed someone to talk to about their grief. He felt sorry for them but hoped they wouldn't expect to replace their loss with him.

A clock chimed midnight and Jason jumped up. "Oh, I have to get some sleep. I'm getting up at six for work. Thank you for the hot chocolate. I have enjoyed meeting you.

He felt ashamed for his actions but hurried out and back to his own apartment. He was angry at himself that he couldn't seem to find a common ground for a discussion with the Dixons. His mind flew around subjects so much that he had a difficult time falling asleep.

# CHAPTER SIX

It seemed to Jason that he had just closed his eyes when his alarm brought him straight up in bed. He yawned and stretched, slowly got out of bed and staggered into the bathroom.

Dressing in a dark blue suit with a lighter blue shirt and red and blue tie, Jason drew on his boots. He snapped on his watch, checked for his wallet and a clean handkerchief and headed for the kitchen.

He remembered he had left his briefcase on a kitchen cabinet at the same time that he smelled the coffee. *God bless the person who invented an automatic coffee maker that could be programmed at night to start working the next morning.* He slipped two pieces of frozen French toast in the toaster and put two eggs on to boil.

While his breakfast was being prepared, he went to his door to pick up the paper which he had delivered. He took off the clear plastic wrapper and sat at the kitchen table to spread the paper out and read. He finally thought to check on the eggs and decided he had let them boil too long, but that was too bad. He'd eat them anyway. He slipped the now cooled French toast into the microwave for fifteen seconds to warm. He spread butter on them and reached for the syrup. Breakfast over, Jason washed what few dishes he had and left them in the drainer to air dry.

He ran to the bathroom to brush his teeth. Returning to the front of the apartment, he put on his overcoat and Stetson, grabbed his briefcase and hurried out. Locking his door he walked quietly down the hall to the elevator hoping he would not disturb any of his neighbors.

In his office, an hour before the others, he concentrated on completing work he had neglected while getting established in The Perfect Spouse. He disciplined his mind to concentrate on the work and not on his impressions of the people he had met at the party.

Grace hurried in bringing a swirl of cold air. She took off her coat and knit cap and hung them up after putting her gloves on a corner of her desk. She placed her purse in a bottom desk drawer and turned to go make coffee. She gave a strangled scream when she discovered Jason standing in the hall.

"What are you doing here this early? You nearly scared me to death. I couldn't imagine how anyone could have gotten in and I sure didn't expect to see you." She sat down to take off her rubber boots.

"I'm sorry, Grace. I've gotten involved in some personal matters and decided I needed to come in early to finish work that I had started. Go on and fix the coffee. I'm having some fresh pastries and fruit delivered in a few minutes. Put them where the three of you can enjoy them." He went back to his office and quietly shut the door.

Jason thankfully completed a quarterly report a local business had hired him to do and to stay on top of their financial affairs. He breathed a sigh of relief and reached for a folder of work that belonged to an attorney in a nearby town.

He lost track of time with his mind so focused on what he was doing. He looked up when someone knocked on his door and then opened it. Grace entered with a mug of coffee, as he liked it and a Bavarian cream-filled Long John. She placed these on his desk then took an apple and some napkins out of a packet.

"Oh, Grace, you're worth a fortune, but you shouldn't have bothered."

"Doing something for you is absolutely no bother. I bet you don't eat properly most of the time with no one to remind you. Do you even shop for groceries?"

"Whoa. At least stop long enough to take a breath. Yes, I shop for groceries and do basic cooking. I had breakfast at six fifteen this morning and it's now ten, so this is good. Thank you."

Grace frowned and leaned against his desk. "There's a Margaret Archer calling and insisting on speaking only with you. I told her that she'd have to make an appointment, but she snorted and hung up."

"Snorted?" he laughed. "Who is Margaret Archer?"

"I have no idea and neither Greg nor Beth can remember ever knowing her or hearing about her. What should I tell her if she calls again?"

"That she has to make an appointment. She also needs to tell you the nature of her business. You know the drill."

"Jason, you have a business to run and need clients, but I had the hair, on the back of my neck, standing up while she was talking. She has an irritating voice. I don't have a good feeling about her."

"Well, if and when she does make an appointment, make sure it's when we're all here. Surely I can protect myself against one woman, but if you would feel better being present, so be it."

"Yes, but she's so persistent and downright rude."

Jason got up and came around the desk to hug Grace. "Thank you for taking care of me. I hope you're not sensing bad when it really isn't there. Maybe it's just because she won't speak freely to you, or better yet, maybe she won't call again." He patted her back and gently urged her out the door. She sniffed and went walking rapidly out and down the hall.

Jason was so engrossed in his work that he didn't stop for lunch. The middle of the morning refreshments Grace brought him was still with him. Grace came back with her outer wear on ready to leave. "Jason, forgive me if you feel I'm too bossy, but I do care about you and want to keep you as healthy as possible. I came in to see if you wanted me to bring you something to eat."

Smiling broadly, Jason got up and hugged her. "Thank you, Grace, and no you're not too bossy. I appreciate your attention and am so fortunate to have you. I can't think of anything I want at the moment. Is there a pastry or some fruit left? If so I'll eat that later."

"There's one pastry that I hid for you and I saved some fruit slices. I'll bring them back to you with a mug of coffee." She scurried out down the hall to happily wait on Jason before she left for lunch. Greg offered to stay behind and take care of the front while Grace and Beth went out. He would go after they returned because he also had a personal errand to run.

Jason stayed so busy that the day seemed to pass quickly. He stretched his tired back and shoulders when Beth came back to tell him goodbye.

"Get home safely, Beth, and have a good night's rest. Be careful. There's still some icy spots."

Greg called goodbye from down the hall and hurried out. He had been leaving right on time for several days, but not doing anything suspicious. Jason smiled to himself and wondered if Greg had met a girl, but then he remembered Greg's sick mother.

Grace finally wandered back to Jason's office. "Aren't you going home tonight? It's way past time to leave."

"My goodness, Grace. Have you stayed just because of me? You need to get out of here before it gets too dark to see well. We're not as busy this time of year as we'll be in the spring, so take advantage of it. We'll hopefully be too busy to breathe in a couple of months. Now get on home."

"Okay. I'll see you in the morning. Goodnight, Jason."

"Goodnight, Grace, and thank you."

"For what?"

"Just being you," he said with a grin and waved his hand to show her to go.

Jason sat in the quiet of the office and contemplated what he should do. Should he continue with the dating agency or let his membership expire. There was a good possibility that he'd meet someone at church after all. But did he really care about finding someone. No, not really. He stood up quickly and shook himself like a dog shaking itself. "Get out of here and stop being such a wimp," he ordered himself.

* * * * *

The next morning Jason drug out of bed and made himself eat a bowl of hot oatmeal with raisins. He dressed warmly because the weather report was warning about a snow storm in the afternoon.

As he turned to lock his door he heard the Dixon's door open. "Hello there," Betty's cheerful voice rang out. "Would you like to come in for a cup of coffee or I would gladly fix breakfast for you."

"That's so kind of you, Mrs. Dixon, but I've already eaten and I must get to work. Thank you for thinking of me."

It hurt him to see the disappointed expression on her face, but Jason felt he didn't really know what to talk about with them. He hadn't really tried to get involved with any specific friends since he moved in Village of Fayette three months before. He truly wasn't searching for a permanent relationship and wasn't interested, or didn't have time, to find people just to run around with them. He hunched his shoulders against the cold air.

Big fat snowflakes started to fall and were beautiful. The sun had not been able to show through the snow and overcast skies which left the mercury lights still on. The lights made a fantasy backdrop for the snow. He smiled as he opened his door and entered his place of business. He turned around to go out again and admire the sign that was recently painted on the window. **Jason McBride, CPA**. Up until a couple of days ago, he had only a hand-lettered sign on a cardboard in the window.

Grace came in right behind him shivering and stomping her feet to get the snow off her boots. They greeted each other and proceeded to hang up outdoor wear and get ready for the day. Grace started the coffee and then jumped in surprise when Jason hurriedly put on his outer wear and ran out.

"Well, for goodness sakes. Where can he be going in such a hurry?" she said out loud. Shrugging her shoulders she continued with her activities for the day.

Beth came rushing in. "Delightful! The furnace is still working. I'm always afraid that it will fail on one of our cold days." she grinned at Grace.

Greg came in with a rush of cold air. "Where was Jason going in such a hurry? He didn't even acknowledge me when I spoke to him."

"I don't know," Grace answered, "but wherever he was hurrying to is his business. After all, he is the boss. Oh, I'm sorry. I didn't intend for that to be so smarty sounding. Truthfully, I wondered myself where he was going."

The three of them settled in to their assigned tasks while Grace answered the ever ringing phone. "No, Ms Archer. Mr. McBride is not here. He's tending to some business outside of the office and I don't know when he'll be back." She listened and held the phone away from her ear, looking down at it as if she thought it might attack her. "I'll give him your message, but you do need to make an appointment."

"Well!" Grace snapped. "She slammed her phone down in my ear. I hope that woman doesn't come in here, but, I'll admit, I'm now curious as to how she looks and what she wants."

"What's bugging you, Grace?" Greg asked sauntering into the front office. "Is that woman a client of ours?" He put emphasis on "that" just as Grace had done.

"Grace looked annoyed. "No, she isn't a client and I suspect she isn't interested in becoming a client. She has called several times wanting to speak to Jason." Grace simpered and said Jason's name as a flirty person might. "She won't tell me what her connection with Jason is or what she wants. She refuses to make an appointment, probably afraid she'll have to part with some money."

Beth came in to stand by Grace. "I hope she isn't one of those poor souls who stalks someone and causes a lot of trouble."

"Who knows," Grace shrugged her shoulders. "I just know she makes the hair on my neck crawl. There's something about her voice that grates on the ears. I can't explain it; I just have a bad feeling about her. I hope she quits calling or will give up and come in."

"Don't let it bother you," Greg patted Grace's shoulder. "Our Jason's a big boy and we're here if he needs us."

Greg and Beth filled their mugs and returned to their desks.

The four of them had their own personal mug, however, in the front office there was a table with a thirty-two cup coffee urn, Styrofoam cups, napkins, cream and sugar both real and substitute. This was free for clients.

To the left of Grace there was a restroom. Beside that was a doorway leading into a large, rectangular room where Greg and Beth had their desks. There was also a long table for their use. In the back of this room was a refrigerator and a microwave. Jason had provided appliances in case any of them wanted to bring a lunch or heat something. Frozen dinner could be cooked in the microwave and potatoes could be baked.

To the far left of this long room was a short hallway leading to Jason's office and private restroom. At the end of the hall was a door leading out to an alley. This door had an alarm on it and would be opened only in emergencies.

Behind Grace's share of space, and beside the long room was a small, privately owned business by a man who cleaned and repaired watches and sold jewelry. This had previously been part of Jason's purchase, but Jason decided to allow someone who needed an income to use it for their business.

Franklin Shackelford, who was the watchmaker, was a widower with grown children who lived in states too far away to care for him. Jason had learned about him through the church and offered the space to him.

At the back of this small business was a curtained doorway leading to a restroom and a small area holding a twin bed and a bedside table with a lamp. Jason offered for Franklin to keep food in the office refrigerator if he wished. It was Jason's idea to place the bed in the shop in case Franklin needed to lie down and rest. Too, Jason had never learned where Franklin really lived and he was afraid that the old man needed shelter. He had instructed Grace to share pastries, fruit, and any extras with Franklin.

# CHAPTER SEVEN

Grace looked and gawked in surprise when Jason came hurrying in carrying a big bakery box and a bag of groceries.

"What in the ---"

"Never mind, Grace," Jason grinned. "Call Franklin and tell him that I want to see him at two o'clock. He hurried through the front room, into the long room and almost ran to the refrigerator. He deposited some items in the refrigerator and other on the floor beside it. Putting a finger to his lips to show, 'no talking', he motioned for Greg and Beth to come into his office. They hurried quietly after him.

"I'll talk fast. I don't want Grace to catch on, but today is her birthday. I found out by accident. I have a cake, two kinds of ice cream and a gift for her. Let's have a surprise party at about two o'clock unless a client comes in at that time and we have to have it later. After all, it's Friday and we don't have a need to put in long hours at work today."

"Are you sure it's her birthday? She hasn't said a word about it." Beth said with a frown and looked worried.

"Yes. December nineteenth. I happened to look at her application and found it. Now get out of here before she gets suspicious. Keep her out of the refrigerator if you can."

Greg and Beth scuttled out. Greg looked back protesting that he hadn't known about it and had no gift for her.

"She won't expect it," Jason assured him.

Grace was naturally curious but everyone was then acting so normal she decided whatever it was, it was Jason's business. She had called Franklin and given him Jason's message. He naturally asked why Jason wanted to see him, but she didn't know.

The morning progressed as usual with paper work to do and a few phone calls. Jason walked to the front.

"Why don't the three of you go to lunch and I'll keep an eye on things here. Don't rush. I don't want anything now, but I might go out later."

Jason was pleased when Franklin wandered in after the three had left. It gave him time to tell Franklin about the surprise birthday party he'd planned for Grace.

"That's wonderful," Franklin was so pleased he was almost bouncing around. "Grace is such a kind, thoughtful person. She deserves nice treatment."

As the three came in from lunch, Franklin hurriedly excused himself and said he'd be back later. When he returned at two, he was looking so pleased with himself that Grace asked him why he looked so happy. He just smiled, gave a jaunty wave and walked on back to Jason's office.

In a few minutes, Jason called for Beth to come to his office. She hurried back and listened to his instructions. She went back and whispered to Greg who quietly got up and helped her. He picked up the bag Jason had placed on the floor and took out a paper tablecloth with Happy Birthday written on it. There were also balloons and cakes with candles printed on it.

Beth placed matching napkins, paper plates, tableware and cups on the table. She opened the refrigerator and took out the bakery box. She had to make a strong effort to keep quiet when she saw the beautifully decorated cake that Jason had ordered from the bakery. It was a sheet cake, double layer yellow, with white icing. Around the edges were green vines and leaves with yellow roses and rose buds. On it was written HAPPY BIRTHDAY GRACE.

Greg took out two quarts of ice cream from the freezer and placed each one on a paper plate to catch any drips. He opened them and placed an ice cream scoop on the plate beside each one. "Yummy" he breathed in the delectable odors.

Beth turned to give him a stern look. He ducked his head, grinning, and went to the front office to casually get his mug full of coffee. "How's it going, Grace, my love?"

Grace looked suspiciously at him because he looked like the cat that had caught the canary. "Everything's fine and since when did I become your love?" she smiled.

"You've always been a love for all of us," Jason said from the doorway with Franklin looking over his shoulder. The four of them started clapping and singing Happy Birthday to Grace.

"Oh, dear, you've taken me by surprise," Grace sniffled wiping her eyes.

"Don't flood the place," Jason laughed. "Come in here with us."

Puzzled, Grace followed them and then gasped and placed a hand on her heart. She burst in tears. "How--how--" she stuttered. Her eyes grew wide when she saw the cake with ten lighted candles on it and the ice cream. A beautifully decorated box with a huge red ribbon was on one end of the table.

"You deserve this more than anyone I know," Jason told her.

She walked shakily to the table and sat down. She looked at all of them with moist eyes. "How did you all do this without me knowing?"

"That doesn't matter," Jason told her. "Here, open this." He gave her the package.

She opened it and gulped in surprise to find another lovely wrapped box inside. She opened it and found a smaller wrapped box in it. "What is the meaning of all these boxes?" she asked puzzled.

"Don't let it bother your pretty head," Jason smiled. "Just keep opening."

The smaller box had a gift in it. She took it out and again burst into tears. "Jason, you stinker. This is too sweet of you, but I can't take it."

"Well, what is it?" Beth asked impatiently.

Grace smiled through her tears and waved her hand in the air with the contents of the box. "It's a round trip plane ticket to Hawaii and a check for five hundred dollars," she finished breathlessly.

"Consider it an end of the year bonus, a Christmas gift, a birthday gift and whatever. You'll leave on December twenty-sixth and return on January second." Jason said proudly.

"Hooray! You'll be out of the snow and cold weather," Greg was excited for her. "Grace, I didn't have time to get something for you, in fact, I didn't know this was your birthday until a couple of hours ago. I hope you won't be insulted if I give you money to spend."

"Oh, Greg, I can't take your money. Don't be insulted, but you need your money for your mother and your own expenses."

"Nonsense. You'd insult me if you don't take it. I honestly want you to have it."

Grace hugged him. "Thank you, Greg, maybe I'll find something nice to bring back to you."

Beth pushed by Greg. "Remember when I left you two in the diner and ran out for a short time? I went to get this." She held a flat package wrapped in gold paper with a big blue bow, Grace began to sniffle again. Beth smiled, "Now none of that. Just open my gift." Inside was a lovely pale blue silk blouse with tiny seed pearls around the hart-shaped neck line. The long sleeves ended in a wide cuff.

"Beth, darling, it's too beautiful for me. I'm glad the sleeves are long. When a woman gets to be my age we need to hide as much as we can,"

Franklin moved toward Grace. "You don't need to hide anything. A woman like you who is lovely inside and out will outshine all the young chicks." He held out his hand. "I'm sorry I didn't have time to wrap this."

Everyone gasped and Grace sat down heavily. The narrow gold bracelet had two teardrop-shaped Aquamarines on either side of a blue diamond. A delicate gold chain was a safety device against losing the bracelet.

"Franklin, this is too valuable for me. I appreciate the thought with my whole heart, but I can't take this."

"You'll break my heart if you refuse it. I made it for my wife whom I loved as much as one can love anyone else, but she died before I could give it to her. The cancer took her quicker than I imagined. You are a dear friend and I would be honored if you'd accept it."

Grace looked at Jason. He nodded at her. She accepted Franklin's gift with more tears and hugs. "I shall treasure it always. Thank you from the bottom of my heart, Franklin."

"If we don't hurry and eat this, the ice cream will be melted all over the place," Greg sang out as he went behind the table. "Who wants Pistachio and who wants Butter Pecan?"

"Give a scoop of each to everyone," Jason suggested. "Grace get back there, make a wish and blow out your candles. Then you can cut the cake."

"Thank you for everything, my precious friends. And thank you for only having ten candles on the cake. It keeps me from feeling so old," she laughed.

"We didn't want the fire department to be rushing in here on such a cold day and this close to Christmas," Greg joked.

"Greg gore ee," Beth admonished him.

With a mighty breath Grace blew out the candles and pretended to be faint. "I don't know whether to kiss you or kick you, Jason. "I'm already plump enough and now I'll be roly-poly after cake and ice cream."

"No, my dear lady, you're just right," Franklin placed an arm across her shoulders and then, looking slightly ashamed, dropped his arm and came around to the front of the table.

Greg lifted his eyebrows and looked at Beth. She smiled and shrugged her shoulders.

After they had eaten and cleaned up, Jason told them to go home and enjoy an early day. Franklin left declaring that it had been many a moon since he had enjoyed himself so much.

Greg leaned over and whispered to Beth. "How long has Franklin's wife been dead? I think he has an interest in our Grace."

"I don't know," she answered, "and he couldn't find a sweeter lady than Grace. I don't know her age, and I didn't want to ask Jason, but she is still very pretty. She has such a sparkling personality and is very loyal."

"I would guess her to be middle sixties," Greg told her. "Wouldn't it be great if the two of them found a lasting relationship?"

Grace made everyone take a piece of cake home for later. The rest was wrapped and left in the refrigerator. The ice cream was returned to the freezer for another day.

"Brrr. Why do we enjoy such cold food in bitter cold weather?" Grace shivered as she prepared to leave.

"I don't know who invented ice cream, but it gets better and better. I, for one, can eat it any time. All of you, get out of here. Have a wonderful weekend."

Jason locked up and bid everyone a cheerful goodbye.

# CHAPTER EIGHT

The weekend was quiet because everything was shut down due to the blizzard that swept through the Village of Fayette. Business people, police and other citizens, who talked to each other, agreed that it had been many years since they had such a severe winter.

By Monday the road crews had cleared the main roads and opened a few of the side streets. Jason called his three employees and told them to wait until the next day to come to work.

On Tuesday Jason took his time fixing blueberry pancakes, sausage and scrambled eggs. He drank two cups of coffee and poured the rest in a thermos to take to work with him. With Grace preparing to leave, he wasn't sure there would be coffee at the office.

As he locked his door, Betty Dixon stuck her head out of her door and called to him. "Good morning, Jason. You work too hard. We never get to see you except in a passing blur. Please say you'll come for dinner tonight. We would love so much to have you join us."

"Oh, Mrs. Dixon, I don't want to be any trouble. I usually pick up a take out to bring home with me or just have a sandwich."

"Absolutely no trouble. I already cook for us and what's one more."

Jason recognized that she and Tony were lonely and missed their children.. He really didn't want to get involved or feel obligated, but he was too kind to keep turning her down. "Okay. It'll be my pleasure to join you. What can I bring?"

"Just yourself at seven. I'm so happy. Tony," she yelled as she stepped back into her apartment. Jason heard her saying. "Jason's going to join us for dinner. Yippeee!"

He walked to the elevator feeling ashamed that he had not given them more attention. He should have been more thoughtful knowing how they had lost two sons and now a daughter and grandchildren. *I don't want them to begin to feel that I'll take the place of their children. I don't dislike them, but I don't have anything in common with them.*

Jason smiled when he passed the Head Above The Rest Beauty Salon and Barber Shop. The music was turned on so that it could be heard on the street. "I'm Dreaming Of A White Christmas" played joyfully. "Yeah, sure," he said, looking around at the pristine snow banks. Whistling, he walked on.

He enjoyed greetings and comments from several people as he made his way down the slippery walk. As he passed the hardware store, he could hear, "Joy To The World."

He walked on to work with his chin dipped down in a scarf wrapped around his neck. It was a clear day but bitter cold. Keeping his eyes on the walk and being careful not to step on any obvious ice, he got out his keys to open the office door. To his surprise the door was unlocked. He pushed it open and stopped in amazement.

Greg, Beth and Grace came out of the middle room to greet him. He sniffed the wonderful odors of pine and fresh greenery. There were ropes of garland around the front windows and more around the room. Greenery and holly were arranged artfully in various places. To his left, in the corner, was a beautifully decorated tree about eight feet tall. He felt dumb-founded. He had not thought of decorating for Christmas and hadn't been aware that his staff wanted to do so.

Multi-colored fairy lights twinkled in the garlands around the windows and around the room. A small tree, about twenty inches tall, had been placed in a window with decorations on it and tiny presents wrapped gaily and placed under the tree. Holly had been placed in several spots to make the window more attractive and festive. Cotton had been placed in the floor of the windows to represent snow. Jason began to grin about the cotton snow with so much of the real stuff on the ground outside. He finally laughed aloud. The three breathed a sigh of relief and looked happy as larks.

Beautiful, full poinsettia plants were on all three desks. "When did you wonderful people do this? I'm ashamed that I haven't even thought of decorating and here you've gone all out and done an outstanding job. Thank you so much. I love it."

The three cheered. Greg came over and slapped Jason on the shoulder. "We wanted to do it because you're the best boss anyone could ever have."

"When did you get all this done?" Jason was still gawking and trying to breathe through his surprise and excitement.

Grace walked over to adjust decorations of the big tree. "We did some Sunday afternoon and when we found out you didn't expect us in on Monday, we came in and worked until we were satisfied with our efforts. You won't be able to appreciate the lights on the hedge at the front until after dark." Grace had planned well and the items were donated by them and some purchased.

"I don't know whether to be angry with you or forget it. I told you to stay home on Monday for a good reason. It was too dangerous to be out in the snow and ice."

"Jason," Beth hurriedly said, "did you know the Chamber of Commerce is going to check business places and judge their decorating? There will be prizes and The Blade will take pictures of the winner and do a story on them.

"As far as I'm concerned you three are the winners and the best." Jason swept his arms out. He started walking through the long room and back to his office. He stopped in admiration when he discovered the decorating that had been done to this room. Pine boughs were place in various locations with pine cones and holly. He smiled and walked on back to his office. Opening his door he stopped in surprise and admiration. "You pixies have even worked wonders back here. It's beautiful. Thank you."

On his desk was a big poinsettia. Around the six by four window were garlands and tiny twinkling lights. In the corner, near his private restroom, was a small tree sitting on a table with a skirt of red velvet under it. This tree, too, was decorated. He grinned as he hung up his coat and then laughed aloud when he saw pictures of the staff taped on the inside of his door. Every picture was taken when the weather was hot, when they were on vacation and mostly wearing shorts or swim suits.

At his laughter, Beth and Greg stuck their heads in the door and ask him to share with them.

"Are all of you hinting for a warm vacation, or are you anticipating the summer to come?"

"Neither." Beth chuckled. "We just thought it might make you feel better in the middle of this cold weather to look at some warm pictures."

"It beats a cold, impersonal door," Jason laughed. "Thank you for doing all of this for me. I hope all three of you will have a wonderful Christmas."

"What will you be doing?" Greg asked.

"I think I've been adopted by an elderly couple who live across the hall from me." He didn't explain that he was being nice to them and hoped they'd leave him alone most of the time.

Grace left to answer the phone and came back looking as if she could shoot a lazar beam. "That was that Margaret Archer again. She refuses to leave a message. I still say she gives me the creeps."

"Forget it, Grace. If she needs our services badly enough, she'll let us know." Jason sat at his desk and took a folder from the files to work on.

There were a few phone calls and mail, but no one came in person. The mail held requests from business people in nearby towns for Jason's expertise. The day passed more quickly than they thought possible.

"Jason, is it all right if I leave a half hour early?" Grace asked. "I need to shop for a cocktail dress for a party and buy a gift."

"Sure. Go ahead. I'll close up."

"Bless you, Jason. Goodbye Beth and Greg. Have a good evening."

She left in a flurry of excitement thinking of her plans. Jason told Beth and Greg that they might as well leave, also. Beth had emptied the coffee urn and washed it ready for tomorrow. They left amid good wishes and Jason locked up.

As Jason turned to walk to his apartment, he heard someone call, "Hey, Jason. Yoo hoo. Wait up."

He stopped and turned, puzzled to see a woman of late thirties or early forties, with hair flying in all directions, running from across the street toward him. Her calf-length coat was flying open, even in the bitter cold, showing a very short brown skirt and a tan, very revealing blouse. He stood mystified as she rushed up to him and placed a hand on his arm.

"I've had such a time getting in touch with you. My name is Margaret Archer and I've wanted to meet you for a few weeks."

"You're the lady who has been calling and wouldn't tell my secretary the nature of your business or make an appointment. I don't do business out on the street. I shall be glad to be of service if you'll call tomorrow and make an appointment."

"Silly." She laughed a deep, braying type of laugh that made Jason's teeth ache as if someone had scrapped finger nails across a blackboard. "I don't need an appointment. I saw your picture, in the book, at the dating agency and wanted to meet you in person."

He looked astonished at her. She stood about five eight and probably weighed about one hundred ten; too skinny for him. She did have pretty mahogany hair and snapping brown eyes. Her eyes had a strange glow in them as if she had mental problems. Her thin lips and far too much make-up did not make her attractive.

"How did you get the name of my business and phone number?" he spoke angrily.

She belted out another loud laugh. "I liked your picture, as I said, and recognized you one day on the street and followed you to your place of business. It was no problem to find your phone number after that."

"Do you realize this is considered stalking? The people at the dating agency assured me of confidentiality unless I choose to meet someone and tell them about myself."

"Don't be a stuffed shirt. We could have a good time. Wouldn't you like to have dinner together tonight and get acquainted?"

"I already have a dinner engagement and I must hurry. Please don't call my office again." Jason turned and hurried away with her following and trying to talk. He soon walked fast and left her behind.

"You're not getting away that easy. I'll see you around," she called loudly after him causing people to look curiously at Jason and at her.

He trudged on wondering what he had done to attract such a nutty woman; one older than he and certainly not his idea of one he would like.

Jason felt badly that he had nothing to bring to the Dixons for the dinner to which they had invited him. Although he didn't drink, he would have ordinarily brought a bottle of wine, but he had never seen any alcohol in any shape, form or fashion in their apartment.

He liked the older couple, but he was happy with his own company and his work. Betty had a scrumptious meal of pot roast, small potatoes, carrots, turnips, tiny onions and just enough spices to make it absolutely delicious. The beverages were a choice of coffee or tea. Home-made yeast rolls melted in the mouth. Jason relaxed and ate far too much, but it was all so good and Tony and Betty were excellent host and hostess.

Jason did enjoy the dinner and the visit more than he thought he might. In fact, he didn't think of Margaret Archer until he got home about nine forty. *I don't know the woman or anything about her and am not interested in learning. I don't remember ever seeing her before.* At this time, he had forgotten the idea of stalking. He just hoped he had seen the last of her.

*I'm really not interested in meeting a woman for anything permanent. I just thought it would be nice to make new friends by joining the dating agency. I keep remembering thoughts my dear, sweet grandparents left with me. Grandma used to say, "Insurmountable obstacles are opportunities in disguise." She was right about so many things.*

He prepared for bed with a twinge in his heart thinking of his grandparents and his loving mother. He was grateful for the love and care of him they had given without expecting anything in return. He had dearly loved his mother and respected his father, but never had love for him.

\* \* \* \* \*

Jason bounced out of bed feeling rested and invigorated. He looked forward to the day and thanked God for his blessings. His staff had become like family. He felt fond of all of them and knew he had made good choices by hiring them. Today he was only going to keep them long enough to give each one a Christmas bonus and clear some business. Tonight he was going to The Perfect Spouse for a special holiday party.

Greg took the envelope Jason handed him with a thank you. Opening it, he sucked in a deep breath. "Jason, you have been more than generous. I need this immediately to pay some of mother's medical bills. Thank you.

Thank you," he said, giving Jason a hug.

Jason didn't know whether to be embarrassed or not. He patted Greg's back and assured him that he had earned every penny. In his own mind, he decided to keep quietly checking on Greg and his mother to see if they were in desperate need or what he could do to help.

In spite of his father's cruel nature, Jason's mother and grandparents had taught him to be a kind, caring person. He had tried to live up to that even though he was a big, strong man and could have been like his father.

Beth hugged him and stated that she would deposit this in her special account for her wedding. She was gushing with joy every day telling them of her wedding plans.

They were all surprised when Franklin came breezing in with gifts for all of them. Greg and Beth looked at each other and winked when he left a special gift for Grace on her desk. "Please don't open it until you're home alone," he explained. It made them wonder how close the friendship had developed between the two.

Jason had an envelope for Franklin which contained a card and money. Beth and Greg had gotten together and bought him a beautiful sweater from New Zealand. Grace had already given him a package, but none of them, in the office, knew what she had given Franklin.

Franklin gave Jason a desk clock, with a calendar, shaped like the steering wheel of a ship. Greg received an Egyptian amulet on a gold chain. Franklin told him it was supposed to be protection. None of them were superstitious, so, it was accepted as a lovely piece of male jewelry.

Beth received a watch with blue stones for a band and a ring to match. The two of them were connected by a gold chain. Franklin had made the gift with Beth in mind.

After Franklin left, Beth followed Jason back to his office. "Have you noticed how Grace and Franklin look at each other? I think, and I hope, there's a little bit of romance there."

"I noticed today how tenderly Franklin looked at Grace. They're both wonderful people and so kind. I think it would be wonderful if he is interested in Grace. She's such a special lady. It's great to have companionship in later years. So many times older people can't go and do as they did when they were younger. To have someone in the same boat, so to speak, is ideal. More power to them."

Jason walked out to the front and smiled at his staff. "This is the twenty-third, so I'll see everyone back here rested, well and happy on January fifth."

"We're going to be closed that long?!" Beth exclaimed.

"Enjoy it," Jason grinned. "We'll be working many grueling hours when we return. Tax time and quarterly reports for several businesses. Besides, I hear we're supposed to have more snow and bad weather."

Beth was ecstatic when the editor of The Blade came in with an officer from the Chamber of Commerce. "Congratulations on your decorations. We're impressed since you have not been open but a few weeks. You didn't win first prize, but we would like to take pictures and do a write-up. You're an asset to the community."

Jason was speechless. He thanked them and allowed pictures to be made inside and out. He and his staff sat down to answer questions and give an interview.

"Well, children," Jason chortled, "this is great. Free advertisement and you three deserve the credit."

They made sure all appliances were safe from fire and cleaned up food crumbs so that unwanted guests, creepy crawlies, wouldn't come in over the holidays. They left wishing each other a Merry Christmas and a happy New Year.

# CHAPTER NINE

At home Jason argued with himself whether he would go to the dating agency party or not. He finally decided to give it another try. Dressing in grey wool slacks and a burgundy sweater, with his usual boots, he got in his car and started out. He was pleased to be greeted by Jenny Carson and Gary Beaumont when he entered the building.

Jason accepted a mug of hot, spiced cider with a small candy cane standing up in it. He shook his head at the offer of sweets. He turned so quickly that some drops of the hot cider jumped out of the mug on to his hand when he heard a screeching voice. "JASON! I knew we'd get together tonight."

Gary and Tony Petrillo flanked Jason as Margaret Archer ran up and hugged him. Before he could dodge her, she had kissed him full on the lips. "Couldn't stay away from me, could you big man?"

"Margaret," Jenny admonished her. "Give the poor man a chance to at least get in. Maybe he's meeting a special lady tonight."

"Oh, no. Tell them, sweetie. We're going to be together tonight."

By then, Jason had gotten his mind and tongue untangled. "I'm sorry if you had any idea that we would be together. I don't even know you and only talked to you a couple of minutes when you waylaid me on the street. Excuse me."

Jason moved as if he were going to leave, but Gary and Tony each took an arm and firmly marched him away from

Margaret. They were joined by Nigel Scovell. Nigel spoke low to Jason. 'Steer clear of that woman. She is so man crazy that she turns all of us off. She had a few dates when she first joined, but people have learned to be busy when she comes around."

Jason smiled at him and inclined his head. *The last time I was here, and met Nigel, I knew I was going to like him. I must get into the bookstore and video shop he owns.*

"Thank you, but I really don't know her. She's been calling me at work, and when my secretary asks for a name and an appointment time, this woman refuses both. I will be very happy if she'll just leave me alone."

"She won't, but she'll lose interest when someone new comes on the scene. A few of the men did date her once each and came back feeling as if they'd been in a war." All of the men laughed as others gathered around.

Jason turned when someone timidly touched his shoulder from behind. He turned courteously and came face to face with the woman who had asked to meet him. He recognized her from her picture and video.

"Hi, I'm Rose Schilling. I just wanted to introduce myself and welcome you to our group."

"Thank you, Rose. I'm Jason and I appreciate your kindness. I hope to meet a lot of nice people, but I'm not interested in a long-term relationship."

"Neither am I. It's just nice to met new people," Rose said shyly. She turned as two women joined the group. "Oh, Jason, this is Rebecca Glover and Annalea Porter. Ladies, meet Jason."

The group was having a friendly discussion when they were interrupted by Margaret Archer.

"Move aside, girls. I saw him first and this man is mine," she giggled, trying to act much younger than her early forties.

"Ma'am, I'm my own man and I sure don't belong to anyone." Jason spoke politely while removing Margaret's clutching hands from his arm. "I don't know you, but I am trying to learn more about these lovely ladies." He emphasized the word ladies. She grabbed his hand and held on.

"You'll know a lot about me after we've had our first date. I know a lot of good-time places to go and I promise you that you'll not be sorry."

"Margaret, are you so dense that you can't hear the man say he isn't interested?" Nigel moved to stand between Jason and Margaret.

"He's just being cute so I'll be more captivated," she giggled.

"Truly ma'am. I'm NOT interested." Jason turned his back on her.

"Poo. You're just pretending to play hard to get so I'll be more drawn to you. Come on, handsome. Let's dance to this lively music." Margaret grabbed his hand and tried to pull him to a place that had been cleared for dancing.

"Ladies and gentlemen, I'm sorry, but I'm going to have to leave." Jason spoke firmly and tried to go to the room where the coat had been left.

Joseph Harper had been observing the conversation and now stepped up to the group. "Hello, everyone. I hope you're enjoying the evening. Jason. That is your name, isn't it? I'm sorry, but I meet so many people it's difficult to keep names in mind. May I talk to you privately? I didn't get a chance to get better acquainted when we met the first time."

He walked off with Jason thankfully walking beside him. "Mr. Harper, I've always been courteous to ladies, but that --- person doesn't seem to want to understand that I'm not interested in her. She sure comes on strong." Jason smiled weakly.

"Yes. Well, Margaret is lonely and eager for companionship. She doesn't seem to realize that she is actually pushing people away from her. If she would make friends with some of the ladies and maybe be invited to go on double dates, I think she'd be much happier. I'm sorry, but I may have to ask her to withdraw her membership."

"Oh, sir, don't do it on my account. I can keep avoiding her and she'll soon leave me alone. I've made friends with some of the gentlemen and they've been good to intercede."

"Jason, it isn't just because of you. We've had other complaints. But enough of that subject. Let me introduce you to some really nice people. You were talking to some of them before you were interrupted. Tucker, come here, please, and meet our newest member."

A man, looking to be in his late twenties, walked to them with a big smile and held out a hand to Jason.

"Jason, this is Tucker Weinstein. Tucker, help me make Jason feel at home and see that he get refreshments, please."

"My pleasure." The young man turned pale blue eyes on Jason. Eyes so pale blue they almost looked silver. His skin was so tan that Jason thought he probably got it in a tanning machine. He was the same height as Jason, but more slender and not as well built. His blonde hair was almost silver and had a slight wave in it. His black, wool slacks and pale blue sweater were ideal colors on him.

Tucker and Jason joined a group which was nibbling on refreshments and enjoying getting acquainted. Jason decided that he really liked these young men. He had never "buddied" around with other young people. First because of his father's reputation and then because his grandparents didn't encourage it. They were careful to keep him with them, loving him and helping him grow and mature.

In college he had not had enough self-confidence to get close to other students. He concentrated on studying, making good grades and visiting with his grandparents as often as he could. Out of college, he was too busy establishing a business and trying to make a home with Linda.

When Jason met Linda Ann Preston in college, he was too shy to make much of an impression. Linda had been observing him and liked what she saw and learned about him. After a time, they began to date and Jason learned that Linda truly loved him and was willing to build a future with him. He loved her with his whole heart. They attended church together and enjoyed many of the same activities. Most of all they enjoyed furnishing a home and planning for the future. For the first time in his life, he felt he had someone for himself and a reason to be content. Until the home invasion.

\* \* \* \* \*

Jason had relaxed so much with this lively group of young people that he temporarily forgot Margaret Archer. A few women had joined the group of men and they were laughing and telling of funny experiences. Jason kept looking at Rose and thought he might try to get to know her better after the holidays.

Suddenly his arm was jerked so hard that he almost lost his balance, grabbing hold of Gary kept him from falling. In fact, Gary saw him totter and reached out to catch him or he would have gone straight over. Perplexed, he looked around to see Margaret Archer grinning and rubbing up against him like a cat wanting attention. Jacob Openheimer scolded her for being so brash. Nigel and Tucker suggested that she go find someone in her own age group. She had answered that men her age were stuffy and boring and had never learned how to entertain a woman.

Although Jason did not care for Margaret, he didn't like the idea of being hurtful or rude to anyone. He took his hand to remove her hand from his arm, but she grabbed his hand as if she were drowning and needed him to save her. He did not smile. "Margaret, I appreciate you finding me interesting, however, I did not join to find a romantic companion and I sure don't do one night stands."

"In other words," Nigel broke in, "get lost immediately."

Margaret pouted in what she probably thought was sexy and would not leave Jason alone. "Give me a chance, Jass. If you'll get to know me, you'll be glad you did."

Gary stepped between Jason and Margaret. "How many times and how many ways does the poor man have to tell you that he is not interested?"

"But he would be if he'd only give us a chance and let us have a date."

"He's not interested!" Gary, Nigel and Tucker spoke as one. They then looked at each other and broke out laughing.

Joe and Elaine Harper had been observing the group and walked over to them. "I'm so happy you young people have made friends and are enjoying the evening," Elaine gushed.

Mark Clark had been quiet until now. "We really would enjoy the evening if Margaret would go away and mind her own business. She can't even be insulted. Sheesh. What a hard-headed woman."

"Margaret, I'd love to talk to you," Joe said. "Please come with Elaine and me." He smiled and placed a hand on her back to gently encourage her to walk to a side room with them. The group breathed as if their lives had just been saved.

Jason excused himself. "Ladies and gentlemen, I've enjoyed the time with all of you and I hope we can get together again. I'm getting out of here and going home. I told you how she got my name and place of business, but I hope she hasn't learned where I live. In a way, she scares me."

Jason got his outer wear and left in a hurry while the others were telling each other goodnight. He glanced back to see Rose Schilling trying to walk carefully across the slick sidewalk to her car. "Hey, Rose. Let me help you." Jason walked back to her and held out an arm for her to hold and escorted her to her car. "Get home safely," he said as he helped her into the car.

"Thank you so much, Jason. I'm sorry your evening was ruined by Margaret. We've all learned to dodge her and be too busy to go with her. When she first joined, a couple of the men dated her, but none of them want to go out again and they've warned everyone else. I feel sorry for her, but she's her own worst enemy."

"Yes, I feel sorry for her, too, but I have too much to worry about without Margaret. Maybe I'll see you again soon, Rose. Goodnight." He shut her door and stepped back from the car as she slowly and carefully pulled away from the curb.

Turning to go to his own car, he saw Gary helping Rebecca to her car. Smiling to himself, and whistling, he got in his car and headed home.

* * * * *

Christmas day was quiet. Jason thought of the times his mother baked special goodies and decorated the house while they sang together. Then his thoughts turned to his precious grandparents and how they had tried to make all the holidays pleasant for him.

He didn't go out except across the hall to the Dixons just long enough to give them a fifty dollar gift certificate to a wonderful restaurant and a coffee table book on day-long trips in the area. They gave him a DVD of some of his favorite songs. Tony had asked him previously what he liked, but he had forgotten it. Betty had knitted a beautiful cream and gold sweater for him.

He was beginning to feel fond of the older couple and told himself he must give them more attention. He just hoped they wouldn't try to replace their children with him in their hearts.

It felt good to stay in bed the following morning and be lazy. His mind began to whirl with plans for the business. He finally thought of the dating agency and again argued with himself as to whether he should continue his membership or not. Later in the day he determined to continue and meet more members. He hoped some of the men would like to golf when the weather was nicer.

# CHAPTER TEN

December twenty-seventh brought another snow. Jason was glad that he did not have to get out in it. Still in his pajamas he eased the door open to get his paper, hoping he wouldn't get the attention of the Dixons. He liked them, but didn't want company this early in the morning.

Back in the small kitchen he poured a second cup of coffee and sat down to open the paper on the table. Headlines on the bottom of the page jumped out at him.

## BODY OF WOMAN FOUND IN DUMPSTER

Not everyone enjoyed Christmas. An unknown woman met with an unfriendly person either on Christmas day or yesterday on the twenty-sixth.

The body of a yet unidentified female was found last night by the men picking up garbage from dumpsters around the Village. As the truck pulled up by the dumpster back of the Pharmacy, one of the men noticed what looked like fingers hanging on the edge of the receptacle. A closer look proved to be the hand of a nude body.

The face was too contorted to make an identification. Police Chief, Aaron Mason, has requested help from the public in identifying the woman. She has mahogany hair and brown eyes; five-eight and about one ten. He would appreciate any information on her name, where she lives and any relatives. Your cooperation will be appreciated.

Jason scanned the article and then read it in detail before the shock of recognition hit him. Could it be ---? He sat spell-bound for a few minutes and then hurriedly got up and ran to get his wallet. In the meantime he threw on a flannel shirt, a pair of jeans and some fuzzy slippers. He took a slip of paper from the wallet on which he had written phone number of Gary, Nigel and a couple of others.

He looked at the clock before making the call and hesitated wondering if it might be too early. He couldn't wait. He rang the number for Gary.

"Lo," a sleepy voice answered.

"Gary, it's Jason. I'm sorry to call so early, but I just read a disturbing article in the Blade. Do you take the paper?"

"Wha --? Who is this?

"Gary. It's Jason McBride. I have something very important to discuss with you."

"Oh, hi, Jason. Wazup?"

"Do you take the Blade newspaper?"

"Yes, I do."

"Well, I can understand that you haven't had a chance to read it this morning. Are you awake enough for me to read an article to you?"

"Sure. Shoot." He yawned loudly.

Jason carefully read the article. There was such silence on the other end that Jason thought Gary might have fallen asleep and didn't hear him."

"Gary, are you awake?"

"Yeah." He yawned big. "I heard you. So. What's got your knickers in a knot over that article?"

"Doesn't it ring a bell with you? Mahogany hair, brown eyes, five-eight. Doesn't that bring anyone to mind?"

"No. Should it?" Another big yawn.

**Think, Gary.** Mahogany hair, brown eyes, five-eight. Don't you recognize the description?"

"No. Clue me in."

"Margaret Archer!"

"Huh. Why would you think of her?"

"Gary, that description fits her to a T. I wanted to talk to you and see if you think we should go to the police and identify her."

"What do you mean we, white man? I have no reason to go to the police about anything and butt into their business. Besides, that could be anyone."

"Forget it then. I'll call Nigel and see what he thinks. Sorry I bothered you. Go back to bed."

"Wait, Jason.---" He had already hung up, checked his list again and dialed Nigel.

"Good morning, Jason."

"Oh, you have an ID screen, too. I wouldn't do without one."

"It's nice to hear from you. What's on your mind this frosty morning?"

"Have you read the article in The Blade about the female body found in the dumpster?"

"No. I just started reading the paper. Where is it?"

"The right hand bottom of the cover page. I'll wait and give you time to read it."

"Okay. I've read it. Are you asking if I recognize the person? **Wait!** Mahogany hair, brown eyes, five-eight. Wow! Do you think that describes Margaret Archer?"

"I thought it might. My question for you is, should we go to the police and see if we can identify her? Hold on a minute. Someone's at my door." Jason practically ran to the door with his cordless phone at his ear.

"Gary! Good grief. You sure got here in a hurry. I'm on the phone with Nigel." Jason spoke into the phone again. "Nigel. Gary just breezed in. I called him earlier, but he was too sleepy to be interested. Well, what do you think?"

"I think you'd better make a pot of coffee and hold on. I'm coming over, too. The three of us can discuss it. Don't do anything rash. Wait on me." Nigel hung up quickly and Jason turned to Gary.

"Wow. For someone not interested, you sure got here in a hurry, dressed and everything. Nigel's on his way."

"I was afraid you'd do something you'd regret. We need to talk about this."

"Okay. I appreciate that. Let me get some sticky buns from the freezer and make a fresh pot of coffee. I'll put the buns in the microwave to thaw and warm. Or would you rather have bacon and eggs?"

"No. Thank you, though. I usually only have coffee and juice for breakfast and then have a mid-morning snack with a lunch about two in the afternoon. Coffee and buns sound great." Gary shivered. "Winter is just starting and I'm sick of it already."

"I don't care for cold weather either, but at least we have heat and warm clothes. Think of the people who don't have that."

Gary picked up Jason's paper and read the article again. By the time he finished, Nigel was at the door and came in shivering and complaining about the cold. "Brrr. It's freezing my lungs."

"I doubt it'll do that much damage to you. You're not out in the cold long enough for that to happen," Jason laughed. "Here. Sit at the table and I'll bring the coffee and buns."

He placed a washable mat in front of the three of them and sat three tall mugs down. He then placed a platter of the buns on the table and a carafe of hot coffee. Cream and both kinds of sugar were on the table. The three men drank coffee, holding the mug in their hands for the warmth.

"Now," Nigel began. "why do you think any of us should volunteer to identify the body? Suppose it isn't Margaret but someone with the same hair color, eyes, et cetera? The police have been known to jump to the wrong conclusions. By that I mean it's entirely possible they might think one of us is guilty and we're trying to cover up."

"Cover up? Nigel, you've been watching too much television. That makes a movie exciting when the wrong person is charged, but I don't think it happens too often in real life." Jason frowned.

Gary tapped Jason on the hand. "Think, man. A lot of people heard Margaret making a nuisance of herself at the agency party. Someone might assume you'd had enough and got rid of her."

"That's nonsense. No one would think I'd kill anyone, even Margaret, although I bet not many will grieve over her. By the way, does she have relatives that are in the area?"

"No one knows," Gary spread his hands out. "She wouldn't tell about herself. I know she didn't live in the Village of Fayette. She drove in from somewhere nearby, because she said once that she could be home in less than half an hour. I'd love to know what Elaine and Joe said to her when they took her off with them."

"I still think we, or maybe I, should go down and identify Margaret."

"Jason, why don't you call Corella and ask if she' seen the article. The agency people would be the ones to identify her -- if it is Margaret."

Jason took a long breath and looked at each man. "I guess you're right. I didn't care for Margaret, but I can't stand to think of anyone being treated in that manner and no one seeming to care."

"I know what you mean. Are you going to call -- or do you want me to?"

Jason looked at Nigel. "Would you mind calling? I will if neither of you want to, but you've both been members longer than I have."

"Sure." Nigel picked up the cordless phone and took a small book from his pocket. "I brought some phone numbers with me in case I needed them." He called Corella's home phone.

"Corella. Good morning. This is Nigel Scovell. Gary Beaumont and I are at the apartment with Jason McBride. We saw an article in today's Blade that we thought needed some attention." He hesitated. "Oh, you've seen it. Does the description sound familiar to you?" He listened. "That's what we thought. Then I guess you're going to offer to identify her or do you know her relatives that might do so?" He listened to her and then wished her a good day and cut the phone off.

"She's already talked to Joseph Harper and he's going down today to see if it's really Margaret. They'll handle everything and we don't need to get involved at all."

Gary leaned back in his chair. "I know the police will want to talk to all of us that are members of the agency. I frankly don't think it could be anyone associated with the agency. I'm sure she was obnoxious wherever she was. Some big mouth is bound to tell how Margaret acted the night of the Christmas party and how we all reacted to her."

Jason leaned forward. "But none of us have done anything wrong. We have nothing to hide. I, and I know you, had no dealings with her except in the agency. That one time on the street when she chased me down surely won't be of interest."

"Just try to think where you've been the last three days and what times you've been wherever. Think if anyone can vouch that they were either with you or saw you." Nigel instructed Jason and Gary.

"I don't have a good feeling about this," Jason sighed. "Or maybe it's because I'm afraid it might be someone we known from the agency. Poor Margaret. She was so eager to be accepted. She would be mortified to know she was discovered nude and frozen in a filthy dumpster."

"I'm not so sure about that," Gary shook his head. Knowing Margaret she would probably think it was hysterical and love the attention."

Gary and Nigel chuckled at Jason, excused themselves, thanked him for the coffee and buns, and left. After they left, Jason read the article again and felt badly that he hadn't been nicer to Margaret.

She had reminded him of a big, slobbering dog who jumped all over people and couldn't be controlled unless shut up in a room apart from the people. He thought about all he and the two men had discussed. *Could the police suspect one of them. I won't be afraid of that happening because I've done nothing wrong. They're right, though. Innocent people get accused all the time of a crime they didn't commit.*

# CHAPTER ELEVEN

The next day Corella called Jason and informed him that the police had asked all of them to come down to the agency and be interviewed. "We had to tell them who was present the night of the party and what a nuisance Margaret made of herself. How soon can you get here?"

"I need to clean up and dress to go out. I'll be there in about thirty or forty minutes." Jason became angry at himself because of the feeling of fear that washed over him. *Get a grip, stupid. You're not guilty of anything.*

\* \* \* \* \*

When Jason walked into the agency, he was happy to see Mark Clark and Tucker Weinstein together. Not far from them was Gary Beaumont, Nigel Scovell, Jacob Openheimer, William Penta and a man he had yet to meet.

The women were gathered in another group. Jason recognized, Rose Schilling, Rebecca Glover, Annalea Porter and Alice Daniels. He smiled as Jenny hurried to him.

"Jason, what a sad time to get together, but necessary. The police have been questioning us one at a time in another room. They've cautioned us not to talk about Margaret to each other until we've talked to them. Would you like coffee or hot tea?"

"I'll get my own tea. Thank you, Jenny." He turned as Corella and Drew Murray came to greet him. They talked a couple of minutes and then Jason walked over to the table to prepare a mug of Peppermint tea. He dropped a tea bag in the mug and poured some hot water over it. He then added two cubes of sugar. Looking around the room, he discovered coats, scarves, gloves and other outer wear on a long table at the side. He added his clothing to the pile and turned when he heard someone speaking low to him. It was Mark Clark.

"Come on over here, Jason and join us. I know we're not supposed to be discussing the reason we're here, but we need to stick together."

"Is this all of the members?" Jason asked surprised.

"Oh, no. This is only the ones who attended the Christmas party. The police will get around to the others in time. Believe me, they'll find everyone."

As Mark and Jason joined the group of men, Jason looked around to see several people he had yet to meet. Everyone greeted Jason warmly. They were careful to talk of innocuous subjects although they were all antsy to discuss Margaret's tragic end.

"Heads up," William Penta spoke softly.

They turned to look in the direction he was looking. Three serious men were approaching them. Jason, in his nervousness, had a strange desire to laugh aloud. He thought of Jack Webb and James Bond. Two of the men seemed very business-like, and the third one was looking around and grinning at everyone.

"Good afternoon. My name is Irving Snouder, Lt. Snouder. I'm a detective with the police department. This is Detective Maurice Watson and Detective Monroe Boggs."

The detectives were greeted politely even though most of the people seemed nervous to be talking to them. Jason looked at them carefully and tried to look as if he spent time daily answering questions by the police.

Irving Snouder was obviously the SAC. He appeared to be early sixties.

About five-eleven and maybe one ninety. He had brown hair which was receding and mostly grey. His hazel eyes were very keen. Jason felt this man was an excellent detective and would be hard to fool. His grey suit was fitted as if it had been fitted and made for him. A surprising lilac shirt was open at the throat and a white handkerchief was folded just so in a pocket of his jacket. Black shoes with thick rubber soles allowed him to move with little noise.

Maurice Watson was possibly late fifties. His blondish hair was thick and wavy. Green eyes were also keen and showing that he noticed more than one would think. He wore black wool slacks and a red sweater. Black boots finished his outfit. He was an inch or two taller than Irving and maybe the same weight. Even though he was watching everyone and craftily getting a visual reading, he didn't butt into Irving's questioning.

Monroe Boggs seemed to be in constant motion. When he wasn't walking around, he had his hands in his pockets jingling items he carried. He was possible in his late twenties, no more than thirty, about six-two and pushing two hundred. His dimples worked in and out as he looked at every female. His honey blonde hair was sporting a military cut which made Jason wonder if he had been in service recently. Caramel eyes twinkled as if he wanted to burst out laughing. He, too, kept quiet and waited for Irving to finish.

Irving looked around and finally spoke again. "We appreciate all of you coming to talk to us. I realize some that were here at the party are at work and couldn't make it, but we'll talk to them later. I realize you've been talking among yourself, and that's only human nature. I must ask that you not talk any more about the case while you are here. We'll talk to the group and then I have a few names I'll call to talk to privately.

A half hour passed more quickly than the people thought it might. Most of them had already talked to the detectives. Those were excused and six names were called to stay for a while. Jason could not keep from having a sinking feeling when his name was called with Mark Clark, Nigel Scovel, Gary Beaumont, Tucker Weinstein and surprisingly, Rebecca Glover.

The detectives took Rebecca in first. She appeared nervous, but held her head up trying to look as if she had charge of her emotions. Elaine Harper watched her go into the interrogation room and then came to stand by the men who remained.

"I'm so, so sorry that this happened. Margaret was hard to like but I can't think of anyone who would wish her harm." She smiled shakily at Jason. "She was one of the first to join when we opened four years ago. She was intrigued with the name, The Perfect Spouse. She thought we were going to assure her that we would find someone for her. I explained to her that I named the business because I felt that my husband was a perfect spouse and I hoped to bring people together who would find someone and be as happy as we are." She sighed.

Jason realized she was talking non stop because she was so nervous. He smiled and hugged her. "I'm so sorry it happened to anyone, but I'm truly sorry you are being put under stress." She smiled and patted his chest as she turned to speak to her husband.

Joe joined the group holding a mug of hot cider in his hands and tried to change the subject. He recognized that his wife was very upset. "Has anyone heard the latest weather report? The last I heard we could expect to be snowed in royally for the new year."

Tucker chuckled. "Yeah, we might as well live in Alaska. It's always a cold winter here but we've sure had more snow than usual. At least it won't lay on long."

Rebecca walked out of the interrogation room, gave them a shaky smile and almost ran to get a mug of hot cider. Andrew stepped up and put a comforting arm around her shoulders. "Was it rough on you, Becca?" he asked compassionately.

"Not really. That oldest one, Lt. Snouder, looks at you as if he knows you're guilty and he's going to force you to confess. Unfortunately, or fortunately, depends upon how you view it, I couldn't tell them much. Someone, I don't know who, had told them that Margaret and I had a quarrel and I had yelled at Margaret. We didn't fight, physically, but I did tell her she was coming on too strong to the men and they would like her better if she were more lady-like. She cursed at me and I told her to just leave me alone and not speak to me again."

Gary chuckled, "And he thought that made you look guilty? He should hear what some of the rest of us said about her, and to her."

"Oh, he didn't accuse me except to ask if I'd ever hit anyone. I told him no, because my parents had taught me to walk away if it was a rough conversation or if I was talking to someone of a violent nature. I assured them I always walked away rather than to continue arguing with Margaret. Poor woman. What a sad thing to happen, and, sad but true, I bet there will be little grieving."

Tony sneered. "More than likely there'll be rejoicing."

"Tony!" Elaine rebuked him. "You're entitled to think what you please, but don't broadcast it." She huffed off to a group across the room and left the little group smiling guiltily at each other.

The men were called in one at a time. Jason was last. The others stayed to give each other moral support.

Detective Watson met Jason at the door and shook hands. He invited him to sit at the table facing Detective Snouder. He sat on Jason's right and Detective Boggs was sitting at his left taking notes and operating a recorder.

Detective Snouder nodded at him and started. "Do you mind if we record this conversation. Talking to so many people we want to be positive that we have correctly what each person said. Too, if you have questions, we want to remember them."

"No, I don't mind," Jason answered, clearing his throat which had suddenly felt as if it were closing on him. He sat up straighter and took deep breaths for fear they would think he had something to hide.

Lt. Snouder stated: "We're continuing in The Perfect Spouse with the investigation of Margaret Archer. It is December twenty-eighth, two thousand eight at two pm. Present are Detective Watson, Detective Boggs and Mr. Jason McBride with myself, Lt. Irving Snouder.

"Mr. McBride, do you understand that this conversation is being recorded and will be used in an investigation of the death of Margaret Archer?"

"Yes, sir. I understand and have nothing to hide."

"Good. How well did you know Miss Archer?"

"Just her name. We are --- we were both members here and I saw her and talked to her a couple of times."

"You never dated her or had any personal contact with her?"

"No, sir. She found my picture in a book here and followed me one day to discover where my office was located. She got the phone number of my business from the phone book and did call several times. She refused to tell my secretary what she wanted or to make an appointment. She accosted me one day on the street and told me how she had tried to contact me. At that time, I had never seen her or knew anything about her. It was my understanding that everything about us would be confidential unless we choose to tell about ourselves."

"Did it make you angry that she had -- let's say, investigated you?"

"No. I wasn't angry, just disturbed that she had tracked me down in that manner. I did not join to find a permanent relationship, which she seemed to be trying to find. I'm fairly new in town and just wanted something to do, other than church, and maybe meet new friends,"

"Did you ever have a confrontation with Miss Archer or argue with her about her behavior?"

"Not exactly." Jason realized the detectives had been told of the behavior of Margaret at the Christmas party.

"Well, exactly what?"

"She seemed to be desperate to gain attention and did come on strong one night during our party. I think some of the others told her to go away. The owners stepped in and asked her to talk privately with them. That's the last I saw of her."

"You never met her outside of the agency?"

"No. I told you I had no contact with her, except the day she accosted me on the street."

"When did you first learn of her death?"

"Yesterday morning when I read it in the paper."

"How did you feel when you read it?"

"First disbelief, then shock, then, I guess grief for her going through whatever she did. I also hoped she didn't suffer. I can't stand to think of anyone suffering."

"How did you know it was Miss Archer when you read the article?"

"I didn't know for sure until I got word from the manager of this agency. The description of the corpse was so familiar that I thought it might be her."

"Mr. McBride, you understand we've investigated everyone that is a member here in hopes of finding a clue to this hideous crime. Of course there is a possibility that it had nothing to do with anyone in the agency."

"I do understand and it should be done."

"Then we can tell you that we found the police report that your father had served a prison term for beating your mother to death, and your wife, your pregnant wife, was beaten to death in a home invasion."

"Yes. I moved here to get away from those ugly, heartbreaking actions. My father had been abusive to both my mother and me. At the time I was just hurting, but as I matured, I, for a short time, hated my father. I decided, and have tried hard, to be a different and better man than he was. I was only five when he killed my mother. It was a bigger heartbreak when my precious wife was killed. I was almost ready to take my own life when I was informed that she was carrying our first child. She was four weeks pregnant. I loved her with my whole heart and would have welcomed a child with a heart full of love."

At this point Jason broke down and shed a few tears. The detectives kept quiet and allowed him to compose himself.

"Gentlemen, I shall apologize," Jason said quietly. "It is still a sensitive subject to remember the horrendous death of my beautiful wife. She was a gentle, compassionate person, who loved her Lord, and would never have done anyone any harm. It is unfortunate that the murderers have not been apprehended."

"We understand your feelings," Detective Watson said, placing a kind hand on Jason's shoulder. "Did you ever think of taking the law into your own hands and going after the intruders?"

"Truthfully? At the time I found out about the death of my wife, I was hurt and so angry that I'm afraid I would have attempted to do harm to them. But as time went on, I knew my sweet wife would not have wanted me to vent my grieve in violence. We both attended church regularly and had Bible study in our home. To approach violence with violence is not the Christian thing to do. No, I would not try to do anything on my own. That's best left up to the officers of the law."

"Thank you, Mr. McBride. We appreciate your honesty and cooperation. You may go now, but don't leave town until you are told differently. Please try not to discuss this case publically. I realize it is tempting to go over know facts and speculate, but you never know who is listening or who will tell something in front of the criminals and block the investigation." Lt. Snouder stood to shake hands with Jason as did Detective Boggs and Detective Waton.

"I understand. Thank you gentlemen. If I can be of any assistance, please feel free to call on me. I don't know what I can do, but I shall be happy to cooperate." Jason walked thankfully out of the room.

He was met in the outer room by Gary and Nigel who immediately questioned him as to what was said. He told them briefly what he could without being obnoxious and refusing to talk about it.

Tucker joined them, venting his frustration. "I don't know why they wanted to talk to us. Neither of us had ever dated Margaret. She was too old for me and I didn't like her anyway. I wouldn't have dated her under any circumstances."

"Maybe we shouldn't talk so much about her because it might give the wrong impression. The police might think we have something to hide and are nervous. Let's talk about the big game between the Ohio Buckeyes and Indiana Hoosiers coming up," Jason suggested. The men walked to get mugs of hot cider.

"Ohio will walk all over Indiana," Gary strutted. "I'm willing to put good money on the Buckeyes for this game. Who wants to take me up on it?"

"Not me," Jason smiled. "I'm too chicken to bet on anything. I've never been lucky. You may be right though. The Penn State Nittany Lions whipped the socks off the Hoosiers the last game they played. If I bet any at all, I'd put money on the Tampa Bay Buccaneers beating the New Orleans Saints next weekend. The Bucs have a score to settle and they're primed and ready for bear. That'll be a lively game."

Nigel sat his mug on the table. "Sorry fellows. This is all very interesting, but I think we'd better clear out of here while the getting's good. We've answered all their questions and we've all been told not to talk about the homicide. We'd better leave before someone decides to talk too much and cause the police to be suspicious about us." Jacob had joined the group and spoke with authority. "I agree" As a practicing attorney, he knew how circumstantial evidence could convict someone.

The men quickly wished each other a happy new year and left. The women followed behind them. They would have liked to talk to the men, but none of them built enough courage to join the group of men. They were all cautious for fear the men would think they were like Margaret -- eager to be in their company.

# CHAPTER TWELVE

Jason parted from the group and decided to walk a bit in the crisp, cool air. He thought the lovely village looked like a Norman Rockwell painting with all the holiday trimmings and the snow. As he walked, snow began to gently fall in big, fluffy flakes. He knew this meant there would not be much snow. The mercury lights began to come on in the gathering dusk, and, with the snow falling in front of the lights, he thought that now it looked like a Thomas Kinkade painting. This gave him a warm, happy feeling.

He looked appreciatively at the big, old hotel built as a masterpiece of Victorian architecture with elaborate wedding-cake trim, soaring columns and a stained-glass cupola. Other than the Senior Center, this was the social center. Many wedding receptions, formal balls and proms as well as arts and craft shows had graced the old building.

In the cold winter weather the flower beds were bare and the vines of the rose bushes looked lonely. He visualized the grounds next spring and could hardly wait to see all the beauty that he knew was there. Again he thought of how he would like to own his own property and raise flowers and flowering shrubbery of his own.

Jason crossed the street and headed back to where his car was parked. He passed a bank, mentally reminding himself to go in and check on his savings account. Next was an insurance agency, a department store and ladies boutique. There was an alley and then a hardware store. Next door was a café and then a mom and pop grocery.

He momentarily felt a sense of disorientation thinking of his family and his home town, but quickly shook himself out of that as he reached his car and unlocked the door. He got in, started the motor, and sat for a moment giving the car a chance to warm up.

\* \* \* \* \*

The new year came in with a blizzard. There were a few small parties held, but, for the most part, people stayed in the comfort of their own dwellings. The fire department did have a fireworks display at midnight. Several people could see this from their own homes. A few had invited friends to join them. Jason stayed in his apartment and was glad for the warmth and comfort. It was going to be long weekend before he went back to work.

He made up his mind to go to a real estate office and look for property during the months of January. He wasn't in any hurry to purchase a home as long as it was cold and a chance of snow. He did want to be aware of what might be on the market, in or near town, that would interest him.

January second, two thousand nine and Jason didn't want to get out of his warm bed. *I'd like to have a dog, but what would the poor thing do all day while I am gone? I guess I could take him to work with me. Nah. It wouldn't be fair to the animal. Scratch that bad idea.*

The weekend went quickly. Monday, January fifth quietly crept in. Jason quickly ate scrambled eggs, sausage and thawed-out frozen biscuits for breakfast. There was butter and blackberry jam for the heated biscuits. He thankfully poured the coffee and was glad he had taken his grandmother's Mr. Coffee before he came to Ohio. Cleaning up the kitchen, he listened to the news and weather report. No new snow predicted and the local roads had been cleared. Deciding to take his paper to work with him, he folded it under his arm, picked up his briefcase and left.

Stepping out into the cold, he shivered and pulled his scarf closer around his mouth and lower part of his face. He knew he was early and planned to start the coffee for his staff and make sure the building was heated.

Much to Jason's surprise, Beth had already arrived and had the coffee going. The glorious heat was going strong. He hugged her and asked about her holiday. She was thrilled and excited talking about her coming marriage. While they were talking, Greg came rushing in bringing a gust of cold air with him.

"Brrr. I'm glad to see you two. I hope you both had a good holiday." Greg spoke haltingly as he peeled off an overcoat, a big, heavy sweater, fur-lined gloves, boots and aviator cap with ear flaps. He sat down and looked at them with a friendly expression.

"Goodness Greg. You're dressed like you think it might be cold," Jason teased him. "Here, get some hot coffee down you."

"When I warm up I'll talk sensibly with you. At the moment my tongue and teeth feel as if they're frozen."

"Yes, Greg, I had a wonderful holiday," Beth told him. "Darrell and I went to a movie in Maumee and ate a huge lobster dinner at a too pricey restaurant. We spent the whole day together since we had to drive a distance. Another day we looked for a china pattern that we both liked and visited with both sets of families. I must admit, though, I'm glad to be back to work."

"I bet friends of yours will give you a shower or two," Jason stated. "You can at least give them an idea of what you'll need or want for your new house. Are you registered at stores where people can get an idea?"

"Yes, I'm registered at Bed, Bath and Beyond, Gem Love Jewelers and Macy's."

Greg turned quickly. "Hey! I miss Grace. I hope she had a wonderful time in Hawaii. Too bad she has to return to cold, snow and icy winds."

"At least she had some warmth and pleasure for a few days. Grace is one who deserves it," Beth explained. "Jason, did you know she took care of her invalid parents and then her husband's parents until they all died. Then her husband had cancer and died slowly. She faithfully cared for him until his last day. She also volunteers at the Senior Center and with the elderly activities at church." Beth gripped a mug of hot coffee and shared the information.

"No, I didn't know all of that. I know she's a special person and thinks of others before herself. Well, children, let's have a short confab and discuss what we're going to be covering the next few days. It won't be long until we'll be climbing out from under tax forms and pressure from anxious people."

The three of them sat at the long table, in the center room, and discussed business for at least a half hour. Franklin came in, got a cup of coffee and talked to them for a few minutes. They asked him about his holiday.

"I had calls from each of my children and visited with some old friends. My church had a beautiful Christmas program that I truly enjoyed," Franklin shared with them. "Now I hate to come back to work, but I have several repairs to do for customers. I'll be glad to see Grace and hear about her trip. Will she be in tomorrow?"

"As far as we know, she'll be home tonight and will be at work tomorrow," Jason answered him. "We all want to hear about her trip."

Franklin left to go to his shop and the three got up to refill coffee mugs before going to their own space to work. Jason was relieved when neither one of the others mentioned the death of Margaret. He had not told them about the dating agency and meeting Margaret, but he felt sure they had read of the strange death. He was glad he didn't have to talk about it.

The next morning Grace was there before any of them. She was bubbling with joy. She hugged each one that came in and told all about her trip. Her pictures would have to wait until they were developed. She had gifts for all four of them.

She gave a coffee table book of plants and flowers of Hawaii to Jason. Greg got a colorful shirt and a CD of Hawaiian songs by Don Ho. Beth was given a beautiful necklace of tiny shells with a matching bracelet. Her gift to Franklin was a small bag of tiny tools that were used to work on watches and jewelry. She also had a Hawaiian shirt for him.

They worked diligently to take down the decorations and clean up the office without wasting time.

The week was uneventful. Jason was on pins and needles for fear someone would mention Margaret's murder and was so relieved when each day passed and nothing was said.

* * * * *

Jason went to a party at the dating agency the next Saturday. He was pleased to discover a few new members. He was introduced to Curtis Warren, Steve Nighthawk and Lisa Madison.

Several of the men and a couple of women were in a group welcoming Curtis Warren. Someone asked him what he did for a living.

"I'm a PJ," he grinned.

"You're pajamas?" Gary asked with wide eyes.

Everyone laughed. "No," Curtis laughed, "I'm a pararescue jumper."

"Okay. Explain." Gary said.

"When I was in the Marines, I flew a lot and was trained as a parachute jumper. Now that I'm out of military service, I wanted to continue to serve my country in some way, therefore, I joined this rescue agency and have been kept busy."

William Penta asked, "What kind of work have you been doing around here?"

"Do you remember reading, or seeing the news on television, about the bridge that collapsed throwing cars, buses and people into the river? There were a few animals in some of the vehicles. We flew over and parachuted out on a long line to lift people and animals to the bank to safety.

There were a couple of ambulances standing by to take anyone to the hospital that was injured."

I remember reading about that," Nigel interjected. "In the article there was also a reference to HALO connected with your work, but I couldn't understand what it meant."

"Sometimes the plane has to fly higher than usual. We jump but don't open our parachutes until we're very low. HALO means high altitude, low opening. We learned to do that in military service when we had to jump in behind enemy lines to rescue some of our people. We also have a DZ which is a drop zone in sight. That means we aim for a specific spot, or zone, to land."

"I'm very impressed," Jason said. "We're glad to welcome you, Curtis and hope you'll be happy here."

Jacob Openheimer brought a lovely young woman to the group. "People, this is Lisa Madison. She's a psychologist and I should have introduced her as Doctor Madison."

Lisa had black hair hanging like a sparkling waterfall almost to her waist. Her black eyes and olive complexion with a very kissable-looking mouth, were eye-catching. She laughed easily and was very personable. Rebecca came to invite Lisa to join the group of women.

Jacob told the group. "She's a humble person and one would never suspect what a wealthy, important family she comes from."

"Who is her family? I must have missed something, because I don't remember anything about her. How long has she been here in the Village?" Tucker asked.

"She's only been here less than a month and I knew about her through a cousin who works with her brother. Her grandfather was the Governor of the state, where they live, and now her father is the Governor. Her oldest brother is the State's Attorney, an uncle is a federal judge, and her younger brother is the District Attorney in a county here in Ohio. Lisa first got a law degree and then decided that she'd rather help people in trouble before they were in deeper trouble. Her college roommate, whom she loved like a sister, committed suicide because of domestic abuse. Lisa was devastated that the girl had not confided in her. Her mother was some royalty of some kind and left millions of dollars to her children when she died of cancer. You'd never know it when you get to know Lisa. She's a very down to earth person."

Jason looked around hoping to meet Steve Nighthawk. His purple-black hair and obsidian eyes with smooth bronze skin was proof that he was Native American. He was tall, taller than Jason, with a well developed body which showed a strong, healthy man. Jason was disappointed that he had already left.

* * * * *

The following week, Jason stopped by a real estate office which was a few doors from his office. He explained that he wanted a three bedroom, two bath house with a nice lawn. He explained that he wasn't interested immediately, but wanted to know what was on the market. If one wasn't available at the present time, his name could be kept on file in the event that something did open. He hoped to buy in February, not later than March, if possible.

Robert Dawson, the real estate agent, took Jason to view the house he had seen and thought he might like. It looked good outside, but there was too much work needed on the inside. Jason said that floor plan was what he had in mind, but not that particular one. He returned to his office prepared to work late to make up his time out of the office.

Jason drug home late, tired, hungry, cold and feeling plain blah and miserable. He hoped that he was not coming down with the flu. He lackadaisically got his mail out of the box and went on up to his apartment. He shook off his outer clothes, leaving them where they fell, and pulled off his boots. He crashed down on the living room couch and pulled an afghan off the back of the couch over him. It was one his mother had knitted and he treasured it. He woke later with a stiff neck, but feeling a little better. It was almost nine o'clock.

He turned on lights and staggered to the bathroom. After he washed his face and hands, he started to the kitchen to fix something to eat, although he wasn't hungry. First he decided to put on flannel pajamas and get comfortable. He heated a can of chicken noodle soup and made a bologna and cheese sandwich. He ate the soup, but only took about three bites of the sandwich.

He ate slowly while watching the ten o'clock news. He cleaned up after himself, hung up his clothes and started back to the bedroom. It was then he saw the mail he had thrown on the divider between the kitchen and living room. He picked up the mail, sighed deeply, and sat on the couch to peruse it.

Nothing of interest. Letters from organizations asking for donations, brochures of summer vacation spots and a letter. Who in the world? There was no return address which usually meant a begging letter, but he opened it anyway. He was startled.

"Jason, Forgive me for writing to you in such an informal manner when we haven't been introduced. I was visiting with my cousin during the holidays and saw you when I was a guest at The Perfect Spouse. She wouldn't let me introduce myself to you, so I'm taking this opportunity to get in touch. I'm not a member of the dating agency and live too far away to belong even if I wanted to. I would like to know you better and have you get to know me. If you're willing to keep in touch, then answer this letter. If I don't hear from you, I'll understand."

"I'm a high school Math teacher, twenty-seven years old, five-six with chestnut hair and grey eyes. I love sports, reading, cooking and jogging. I have a three year old Bull Mastiff whom I love dearly and have had since he was two months old. I call him the Professor because he looks at me as if he knows exactly what I'm saying and can almost read my mind. He's an excellent guard dog, but can be very friendly once he gets to know a person. I play the piano, organ, guitar and accordion."

"I hope you'll be interested to at least get acquainted. If you decide to contact me, mail a letter to: Candy, Box 501, Findlay, Ohio, 45839. Of course Candy is not my name, but I don't want to give my full name yet until I learn how you feel. I just want a friend with whom I can correspond and not expect a permanent relationship."

Jason rubbed his eyes and across the top of his head. What?? How did this person get his address? He then thought of how Margaret had tracked him down and wondered if he should be frightened. Should he show this to the detectives investigating Margaret's murder? He shook his head, left the letter lying on the couch and went on to the bedroom. He was too tired and felt too miserable to worry about this now. He was afraid he wouldn't sleep, and he did toss and turn, but finally dropped off to sleep.

Jason got up the next morning feeling as if he were floating and wandered to the bathroom. He felt better in a few minutes and decided he wasn't getting the flue after all. He dressed and padded on sock feet to the kitchen. His heavy wool socks kept the kitchen tile from feeling cold on his feet. He ate a bowl of Cheerios with a cut-up banana, toasted two pieces of cinnamon raisin bread, buttered the bread, and ate it while drinking a second cup of coffee laced with cream.

He brought the paper in and dropped it on the couch. The letter from the mysterious woman caught his attention. He picked it up and read it through again. He rubbed his head and decided to think about it. He pulled on his boots, put on his outer wear and walked slowly out to go to work.

Jason mumbled a greeting to his staff who were already busy for the day, and walked on down to his office. He hung up his coat, placed gloves, scarf and hat on a small table behind the door, half way smiled at the warm weather pictures of his staff, and sat heavily in his chair.

In a few minutes Grace tapped softly on his door and then stuck her head in timidly. "Are you feeling all right Jason?"

"Yeah," he said with a deep sigh. "I guess I'm all right. Probably the winter blahs. I just don't have any energy or any desire to be here today."

"Why didn't you stay home? We can handle the office for a day or two on our own."

"No. I'm just as well off here and I'll get going soon. Thank you though." He tried to smile at her but just turned up a corner of his mouth.

Grace backed out and walked slowly back to the front. She stopped a moment to explain to Beth and Greg why she had checked on Jacob and what he said. They truly cared for him and wished him well. They quietly went on with their assigned tasks.

Jason was embarrassed to awaken and discover that he had slept at his desk for a long time. Greg and Beth had already left for the day, but Grace tiptoed in to check on him.

"Oh, Grace. I'm so sorry. I don't know what came over me. I've---"

"Say no more. You're plainly worn out and mother nature helps us all heal and feel better after a nap. It's past time to leave, so, go home and I'll leave, also. I hope you get a good night's rest and will come in refreshed tomorrow."

Grace left in a flurry after literally pushing Jason out of the door and locking up after him. She went happily on her way leaving Jason to walk on home. His crock pot had faithfully worked all day to cook a beef stew with vegetables. Jason had a bowl with some heated garlic bread, brushed his teeth and fell into bed.

He awakened feeling much better and eager to be up. He sang in the shower and grinned to himself that this was the only time any more that he sang. He decided to leave early and have breakfast at Marjorie's Café.

# CHAPTER THIRTEEN

"Well, hey, Jason," Marjorie Wakefield, the owner and chief cook greeted him in surprise. "We don't see you in here at this time of day. To what do we owe this honor of your presence?" She kept it from sounding sarcastic by coming from behind the counter and hugging him.

"I just decided that I'm tired of my own cooking. Why don't you surprise me with your most popular item on the menu. Hello, fellows." Jason greeted a few men that he knew from church and the bowling alley. He sat in a booth near the front window.

Marjorie brought him orange juice and a mug of coffee. In a few minutes she sat a platter in front of him that caused his eyes to all but bug out. He blew a whooshing breath and laughed aloud. "Do you expect me to eat all of that in one meal? I never eat much in the morning. Whoooooeee."

The men, closest to him, began to tease him. "Now be a good boy and clean your plate. You want to grow up to be a big, fine man." Everyone in the restaurant laughed.

Jason looked at the short stack of pancakes, 2 sausage links, 2 slices of bacon, a pile of scrambled eggs, hash brown potatoes, slices of tomato and a bowl of grits. He looked around at the laughing men and up at Marjorie standing with her fists on her ample hips. "Well, here goes."

Jason was even surprised when he sat back with a deep breath and realized that he had truly cleaned his plate. Now the waist of his pants felt too tight. The men applauded and slapped him on the back. He grinned and enjoyed the friendship.

"Who's going to roll me over to my office? I don't think I can walk on my own." He looked around as if he were pleading for help.

"There's no hurry. Sit a while and you'll be able to go where you wish," Marjorie told him.

Attorney Maurice Winston slid in the booth opposite Jason. "Good morning, Jason. I've been going out of town for my CPA service and I've been satisfied, but I'm wondering if you'll find time to meet with me and discuss my financial situation. I never seem to have my tax forms ready on time and always have to apply for an extension. It's costing me money that I can't afford."

"Sure. I'll be glad to help, if I can. Why don't you call my office and ask Grace to set up an appointment for you."

Maurice stood up, shook hands with Jason and walked jauntily out. Jason paid for his monstrous breakfast and left a five dollar tip. He ambled out and diagonally across the street to his office.

After being out in the cold wind, the heat hit him like a slap in the face when he stepped inside. He hurriedly took his outer clothing off and turned to talk to Grace. She followed him back to his office.

"Grace, do you know Attorney Winston, Maurice Winston?"

"I sure do. I've known him practically all his life."

"Good. What do you think of him?"

"In what way?"

"He asked me this morning if I would help him with his financial reports and his tax statements. I told him to call you and arrange for an appointment. I'll probably need about an hour with him."

"Fine. He's a good man; hard working, and, as far as I know, honest. His wife died last year after a severe asthma attack. He has two young children that her parents are helping him raise. His own parents died in Ecuador where they were missionaries. They were killed in a battle between tribes."

"Do what you can for him. I'll at least hear him out. Thank you, Grace."

She turned smartly and left, pulling his door quietly closed behind her. At eleven o'clock, Grace came back again with a puzzled expression on her face. "There's a Detective Snouder here to see you. Do you want me to bring him back to your office?"

Jason felt a pang of alarm and then slight anger. *Why is the detective coming to my place of business? Does he think I'm guilty or know more than I told them?* "Yes, please, Grace, show him on back."

"Hello, Detective Snouder," Jason greeted him rising and coming around to the front of his desk to shake hands. "Have a seat. Would you like some coffee?"

"I'd love some. Small amount of cream, no sugar, please," he smiled at Grace who turned reluctantly and left the office. The two men discussed weather, football scores and innocuous topics until Grace had delivered two mugs of hot coffee and some pieces of cake, then left, closing the door behind her.

"Jason, may I call you Jason?" Detective Snouder smiled.

"Of course. I'm curious as to the purpose of your visit."

Lt. Snouder sat back in his chair and placed his left ankle over his right knee. "My partners and I were impressed with you, and after a thorough investigation, we thought you'd be relieved to know that you are not a suspect, not even a person of interest."

Jason stared at him for a few moments. "Well, thank you --I think. Why make a special trip to tell me?"

"We're hoping that you'll be willing to be alert and keep an ear open for any comments from anyone that sounds as if they're hiding something. I don't expect you to become a detective overnight," he chuckled, "but we sure could use a friend inside. People might talk in front of you where they wouldn't in front of us."

"I guess I should feel flattered, but I would not be comfortable playing the part of a spy on the members, or anyone."

"Oh, we don't want you to spy; just listen carefully to comments."

"I won't promise anything, but I will say if someone is obviously covering up or appearing guilty, then I will talk to you about it."

"Thank you. That's all I can hope for. Thank you for the coffee and for your time."

The men stood, shook hands, and Jason escorted Lt. Snouder out.

Jason realized that Grace was curious about the detective's visit, but he was not ready to talk about the death of Margaret to his staff. He had a jolt of surprise when Grace followed him back into his office and leaned against the door.

"I wonder what happened to that Margaret Archer. She hasn't called again and she seemed so determined. Well, maybe she's busy like all of us." She stared at Jason, and when he said nothing, she shrugged her shoulders and left.

Jason felt guilty because he knew Grace was fond of him and what a loyal assistant she was. How could he tell her -- and the other two? *Would they think I was careless and negligent? No. We have a special rapport, both working and personal. Maybe I should tell them. I'll think about it, and pray about it. It might be well for them to know because it's possible they would be able to advise me. At least they'll give me moral support.*

The next morning Jason had decided to confide in his staff. He went in early, but even then, Grace was ahead of him. "Grace, please have everyone meet me at the long table in half an hour, and have plenty of coffee."

Franklin wandered in which, at first, made Jason a little uneasy, but he decided that the older man had been in business for years and would have common sense advice. Too, he was a friend and just as interested in Jason as his staff was.

They were all unsure and uneasy when they first sat down with their mugs of coffee. Jason looked down at the papers in his hands and then carefully placed them on the table. The others began to be afraid he had traumatic news for them. Finally he looked up.

"I've kept a secret and feel guilty about it because I felt insecure and wasn't sure how all of you would feel about me. Although I didn't instigate the situation, and could do nothing about it, I still felt badly." he was silent.

Greg cleared his throat, but didn't follow through with saying anything. Beth looked concerned and Grace unconscientiously reached and took Franklin's hand.

Jason took a deep breath. "Remember the calls from the woman who gave her name as Margaret Archer? I need to start before that. Six weeks ago, I joined a dating agency called The Perfect Spouse."

Greg almost choked on his sip of coffee and started to cough. Beth actually dropped her mouth open and stared. Grace kept Franklin's hand and placed her other hand on his forearm. She looked very concerned. Franklin just waited looking solemn.

"Jason. Why would you join a dating agency? You're a handsome man and have a successful business. Lots of women would be eager to know you better, and I know some in church who are interested." Grace spoke with affection.

"I just wanted to make some friends who didn't know much about me, and I'm sure not looking for a permanent relationship."

"That's all right, son. It's your business. You didn't have to tell us, but there must be a reason why you're telling us now." Franklin looked concerned and spoke encouragingly.

"A very good reason. Margaret Archer had joined the same dating agency long before I did. Even though we are promised confidentiality, she did some unethical digging and found my business phone. She caught me one day after work, on the street, and confessed that she had recognized me from my picture and followed me to the office."

"Well! That's why the snit wouldn't give me her phone number or leave a message," Grace huffed. "I'm glad she was never able to catch you here."

"She, as I said, did catch me one day on the street. I told her I didn't do business on the street and she'd have to tell my secretary what she wanted. She laughed, a crazy laugh, and that very night was so obnoxious at the agency, I almost walked out. Others begged me to stay and they told her to get lost." Here he paused

"A few of the men had dated her at first, but they warned me away from her. It seems she was so man crazy she now caused the men to dodge her and to warn others about her. That night at the agency, she grabbed me like an octopus and I had a time getting away from her. The owners finally asked her to talk to them in private."

"Good. I hope she lets you alone after that," Beth smiled.

"She wasn't in any shape to be an additional bother because on either Christmas day or the day after, she was murdered." Everyone gasped. "She was found nude and in a dumpster behind the restaurant. That's why the detective was in here the other day to talk to me. At first I was a person of interest because someone had told them what a time I had getting rid of her that night. The detectives interviewed everyone that was at the party, and others, too. They finally decided I was completely innocent; at least that's what they're telling me now."

"Well, of course, you're innocent. Any fool would know that," Grace spoke through tight lips.

Beth nodded so strongly that she must have hurt her neck. Greg leaned back in his chair and stared as if he couldn't believe what he was hearing.

Franklin placed a hand on Jason's shoulder. "I'm sure you weren't the only one the detectives were investigating. With a reputation as you tell us she had, I'm sure there were several others under suspicious and maybe some who didn't belong to the agency."

"Yes. Others were questioned and a few of the women were questioned because they had verbal battles with her."

"It's unfortunate that the woman's life ended that way, but knowing you, I'm positive you know nothing about it. You're feeling badly about it, and you shouldn't. You never dated her or had any contact with her except what she instigated on her own. You're a gentleman and a very kind person. You're just feeling badly about the whole situation," Franklin observed.

"It's needless to say forget about it, but I'm glad you told us. Everyone needs a friend who can listen to their heartaches and concerns and assure them of all kinds of support. We love you and admire you and will stand by your no matter what." Grace gave a firm nod.

Beth jumped up and came around the table to hug Jason. "There was absolutely nothing wrong with you joining the dating agency. It's your personal business and I hope you'll eventually meet someone who will make a great and good difference in your life. All humans need someone that they can confide in."

Greg stood, looking worried. "Jason, never hesitate to discuss anything with us. You've been like a big brother to me and I treasure our friendship. I'm sure everyone here feels close to you and wants the best for you. You've told us now -- so be at ease. Try to put it behind you and know we're here for all and any reasons."

"Hey! I know and I do love all of you. However, that's not the most shocking item I need to discuss." He turned to Franklin. "I need to know what a wiser head than mine thinks of this next piece of business."

Greg and Beth sat back down looking at each other and then at Jason. He proceeded to tell them of the letter he received, and even read it to them. "One part of me is curious and wants to know more about this person, but then I remember Margaret Archer and shudder."

Greg had picked up the letter to read silently. He laid it on the table. "I say answer and find more about this person. She doesn't sound like someone who would give you any kind of grief. After all, she isn't close by."

"I don't know. Why would someone who doesn't live here want to get in touch, and at the same time remain detached?" Beth mused.

Grace said nothing but got up and hugged Jason with moist eyes. She sat down again and looked as if she were thinking deeply.

Franklin smiled at him, "Leave it be for a while. It's unfortunate this letter came practically on the murder of the other women. Of course it fills you with questions. I would let it rest for a week or two and then decide what you want to do. Never mind what we think. It's your life, and as the others have said, we all are here to support you in whatever you decide."

Franklin leaned over and whispered something to Grace. She smiled at him with trembling lips. He stood up and walked out without another word.

Jason looked at his staff. "Thank you for your understanding and your support. I value your opinions. Now, we'd better get to work. We have people depending on us."

Chairs scraped as each one stood and walked to their own work station. Jason ambled back to his office and slowly closed his door. He made a valiant effort to keep his mind on business, but couldn't keep from thinking of happenings outside the office.

The remainder of the week went by with no new developments in the murder case. The following Monday morning, Gary frantically called Jason.

"Hey, Jason. Can you please come to the dating agency? I need all the friends around that I can get."

"Sure. What's up, Gary?"

"Too much to tell right now. Please hurry down here."

Jason hung up bewildered, but had presence of mind to call Grace and tell her where he would be. He assured her he was not in any trouble, but was going to help a friend. He was astonished to see police, agency staff, and lots of members in the building when he arrived.

Gary, Nigel and Tucker hurried to meet Jason all trying to talk. "Whoa, whoa. I can't understand if all of you are going to talk at once. Gary, since you're the one who called me, tell me what this is all about."

Gary sat down heavily showing that his legs were about to collapse under him. He struggled for a steady breath and finally spoke. "As you, and the others, know, I don't often sleep well. I have been classified as an insomniac. I get up and either watch TV or read. Last night I decided to bundle up and go for a walk at one in the morning. As I walked past the alley by the hardware store, I heard a woman's voice protesting something and calling for help. I ran into the alley intending to help. I know," he said, holding up a hand when Jason opened his mouth to speak. "I know it was a foolish thing to do. I should have yelled loudly and got a lot of attention. Anyway I did rush in. Yes, I know the old saying, 'fools rush in where angels fear to tread', but I didn't think about anything except some woman needed help."

"Well, that was a gentlemanly thing to do, but very dangerous. You didn't know whether the assailant had a knife or a gun," Jason reasoned.

"I know, but how do you think I would have felt if I had hesitated and found another dead woman?"

"Tell him the rest," Nigel prompted.

Steve Nighthawk joined them and asked permission to sit with them. "Being in law business, I'm interested and would like to help." The four men welcomed him and briefly brought him up-to-date. He had apparently been told of the events surrounding Margaret's demise. They each introduced themselves.

Gary proceeded. "When I yelled, the person swung around to look at me and then dropped the woman like a rag doll and ran. I ran to her, relieved to find a pulse. My continuous yelling had gotten the attention of a foot patrolman and he ran to us while calling for backup. A police car pulled in to the entrance of the alley and two officers got out and ran to us. The EMTs were right behind them. Thankfully the woman was taken to the hospital in time."

"Was she wounded in any way?" Steve asked.

"She had a small cut across the back of one shoulder and the person had attempted to strangle her. The shocking part is that she's one of our members. Alice Daniels."

Nigel made a disgusted noise. "Someone is trying to make a point by attacking women from this dating agency, but, for the life of me, I can't imagine what that point is."

"That's not all," Tucker spoke. "One of Margaret's blouses was found nearby and Alice's blouse was nearly torn off her. He apparently was trying to leave her nude and dead as he had Margaret."

Detective Watson and Detective Boggs moved to this group of men. Det. Watson was tired and angry. "This person is baiting us. He's attempting to commit murder and leave useless clues. I don't know yet what to make of it, except that it proves whomever killed Margaret Archer also tried to kill the Daniels woman. He's a master at baiting us."

Detective Boggs gave a whoop of laughter and slapped his thigh. "Yeah, he's master baiter. Get it? A master baiter." When no one laughed with him, he stopped, getting red in the face. The men, and others around them, were looking at Boggs as if they thought he'd lost his mind.

Detective Watson frowned, pursed his lips, and proceeded to talk to others hoping to get a glimmer of a reason for the attack on Alice. "I'll go to the hospital later and hope Miss Daniels will be able to tell me what happened."

# CHAPTER FOURTEEN

Days went by and still no new evidence in the Margaret Archer case. Members, of the dating agency, began to trickle back in, although many of them were subdued and didn't seem to have the interest they had before. A few went on dates, but, for the most part, they were content to have get-togethers and visit with each other.

Toward the end of January Detective Boggs came alone to one of the parties. The members were polite to him and even included him in conversations, but no one seemed to try to get close to him or know him better. He was probably an excellent officer, but he lacked people skills. He tried too hard to fit in and it turned people off.

February rolled in with cold, brisk winds, but the snows seemed to go farther north and west. A cold rain fell one day and made slush of the banked snow that was pushed to the side of the road and the patches on the grass under trees.

Jason's office was extremely busy. He began to wonder if he needed to hire an additional staff member. Even Grace was doing some of the less demanding paper work and answering questions to the best of her ability.

Jason was pleased that he had built such a good reputation and attributed it to his great staff.

Beth had first talked of a Valentine's Day wedding, but now decided that she would wait until after tax time. She felt that she was practically buried in paper work and didn't want to leave and make it more difficult for her fellow workers. Greg, Beth and Grace had begun to feel as if they were in a family of their own with Jason.

Jason was humbly pleased when Police Chief Aaron Mason not only brought his own business to him, but recommended that others come to Jason. Several people in his church were making use of his services.

At the beginning of the second week in February, Jason picked up the letter again from the woman who had written to him. He read it through twice and then made up his mind to answer it. That night, at home, he sat with a legal pad on his lap and penciled in a copy of what he wanted to say. He wrote, crossed out, wrote again until he was satisfied and then typed:

**Candy,**
To say I was surprised to hear from you is an understatement. I have never contacted anyone, male or female, in this manner before.

I've been a long time answering because I haven't known what to say. You have me at a disadvantage. You've apparently seen me, and found a lot of information about me, and I know nothing about you.

Forgive me if I seem suspicious. You probably have heard by now about the hideous death of one of our female members. She was guilty of stalking men and creating a nuisance of herself. I had never dated her, but I had talked to her and knew who she was. Sometimes it seems unreal to think about what has happened in the past.

I do belong to a church and am content with my lifestyle. I could not be interested in anyone who does not believe and have faith in our Lord. I'm not ignoring people who do not do exactly as I do, but I'm more comfortable with someone who does have a relationship with our Savior.

Yes, I'm curious to know more about you and hope to be able to meet face to face soon.

        Sincerely,

        *Jason*

        Jason McBride

The office was so busy with tax preparations for clients that Jason put the letter out of his thoughts. He had not been to a party at the dating agency for some time, but decided to go on Saturday.

At Marjorie's Café having lunch, he was pleasantly surprised when Tucker and Jacob came in and sat with him. Tucker was laughing so hard that he could not talk clearly for several moments. Jacob was laughing also until Jason began to feel they might be laughing at him. He told himself he was just being paranoid and silly.

Tucker finally got control of himself and between giggles told Jason what he was laughing so hard about. Detective Boggs had invited himself to their Valentine's party. He had flirted with all the women and bragged to any man that would listen. He began to follow Lisa Madison around and trying to get her attention.

Jacob broke in. "Remember Lisa? About five-five, long, silky black hair, green eyes, a ready smile and witty. She was an attorney and decided to go into another field."

Jason nodded. "Oh, yes. She joined after I did. I know who she is, but I've never had a chance to get really acquainted with her."

Tucker hurried on. "She's a psychologist, and, we understand, a very good one. Old Boggs flirted with her until we could see her getting annoyed. Boggs laughed loudly and said, "Hey, Doc. Can you read my mind?" She looked carefully at him and we all waited breathlessly for her response. She gave a little nod and said, "Oh, I tried and then decided it would be a lost cause. All I encountered was a vast wasteland." She then smiled and walked off to talk to some nearby people. Boggs stood there with a shocked look on his face."

By now Jason was also laughing and understanding why Tucker got such a charge out of the story. "What did he do then?"

"He closed his mouth, looked around, smiled sheepishly and quietly began talking to others. He left soon after that. He might be tops in his work, but he sure doesn't know how to win friends and influence enemies."

Jason privately felt sorry for the detective and decided that, if he was present when the man came in again, that he'd make an effort to be nice to him. Jason hated to hurt anyone's feelings.

\* \* \* \* \*

Talking a walk one day, Jason was impressed with the beautiful flowers blooming in the garden around the old hotel. The crocus, corydalis lutea, clematis and snowbells were blooming profusely. The Cardinals were flitting all over the place and a beautiful little blue bird with an orange chest was in most of the trees. He felt the peacefulness of the place and could hardly wait for the roses to bloom with the other summer flowers.

February sixteenth was Beth's birthday. Jason took his staff to a dinner at the hotel and gave Beth flowers and a generous check. She was pleasantly surprised and declared that her wedding money was building. She had received money from relatives and a few friends of the family.

She was bubbling over with joy telling of her wedding plans. Her father would walk her down the aisle. Her two older brothers would be ushers and her one older sister would be her matron of honor. Her younger sister would be a bridesmaid with Rebecca Glover and Cary Aimsley from her Bible class. Tiffany Trump, Clarise Goodson and Glinda Beacon were to be her wedding planners and would take some jobs.

Tiffany and her sister, Alma, would be in charge of the bride's book and see that everyone signed in. Fran Perkins would keep track of presents and make a list of gifts and presenters so that Beth could write thank you notes.

Beth turned to Jason. "I want so badly for you to be in my wedding. If my father couldn't have made the trip, I was going to ask you to walk me down the aisle. I talked to our pastor about it and he suggested that you would be the ideal one to sing. Oh, please say you'll sing."

Grace was beaming at her and finally got to say something around Beth's excited chattering. "Have you and Darrell set a date yet?"

Beth bounced in her seat. "Yes, we've set it for the twentieth of June. This year that's the day before Fathers' Day," she giggled. "Jason, you will sing, won't you? Please, pretty please."

"Since you ask so nicely, how can I turn you down." he smiled at her.

* * * * *

Jason was pleased more than ever about the amount of work he was getting. He had told his staff that a good name and a good reputation was more important than earning a lot of money, but the money was certainly coming in. He felt blessed to know that he had been accepted and taken into the community.

February rolled by and March blew in with a horrendous cold rain storm that flattened blooming flowers and filled ditches, pond and waterways to overflowing.

"In like a lion, out like a lamb," Franklin reminded them. "I heard that all my life. If March came in with storms or bad weather, it meant an early spring. Boy, I hope that's true."

"I haven't heard it, but I sure hope it's true," Greg rubbed his cold hands briskly, hunched his shoulders and walked back to his desk leaving Franklin at the front talking to Grace. He didn't try to hear what they were talking about, but did observe how softly they talked together. Grace had to stop a few times to answer the phone. Franklin finally left.

Greg came hurriedly to the front. "Franklin's gone? Shucks. I wanted to ask him what would happen if March came in like a lamb and left like a lion."

Grace said, "I guess it would mean a late spring and cold until summer."

"Booo", he said and went on back.

Beth began talking about a honeymoon. "Darrell won't tell me where he has made arrangements for us to go. I sure would enjoy a trip to some island where we can swim and surf. At least it will be warm," she shuddered.

Jason had made a couple more trips to The Perfect Spouse and had even invited a couple of the women to dinner and a movie. He had also taken a couple of young women from the church on a date.

He had asked Dottie Cornett to go for a horseback ride on a trail out of the Village of Fayette. The Marshall Merry-weather family had a small ranch outside of the city limit, but close by. Dottie admitted that she didn't know how to ride, but wanted to learn. She would have gladly gone anywhere with Jason.

The following Saturday Jason drove over and picked Dottie up to introduce her to horseback riding. "Jason, how do you know how to ride? Haven't you always lived in the city?"

"Yes, but when I was little, and went to live with my grandparents, they took me for riding lessons twice a week for a long time, I really enjoyed it. Then I guess I got older and life became more demanding. Too, I sang in the school glee club and the youth choir at church. I played basketball and worked on the high school newspaper. I haven't really thought about it, but my grandparents were older when they took me and they sure didn't get any younger. They were probably glad that I developed other interests and they didn't have to drive me for lessons.

They arrived at the Merryweather Ranch and got out of the car. Jason walked over and started rubbing behind a horse's ears. The horse put his head down and rubbed against Jason's chest showing how much he enjoyed the attention.

"Dottie, come on over and get acquainted with the horse you're going to ride."

She fearfully walked hesitantly to the horse and stood right in front of it. "Oooo, he's so big."

At her voice the horse threw his head up and backed up a step. Dottie immediately squealed and jumped back causing the horse to jump.

Jason was trying hard not to laugh. "Dorothea Ann Cornett, the animal doesn't know you're afraid of him. He senses your fear and thinks to himself, 'something to be afraid of? What is it? Where is it? Do I need to run? Running is their first line of defense."

"But he put his head up looking down his nose at me as if he doesn't approve of me."

Jason did laugh aloud then. "He's just trying to get a better look at you.

Notice how large his eyes are and where they're located kind of far apart."

"Why doesn't he just look? Why does he have to look like an old British gentleman sneering at me?"

Jason continued to laugh and then apologized. "Horses have two types of vision; binocular and monocular. Because of the positioning of the eyes, a horse cannot see directly behind him or down below his nose. The binocular vision is for long distance. He can see with both eyes at the same time. He has to raise his head to focus on close objects and lower his head to see faraway objects. Monocular vision allows the horse to see areas on both sides of his body. The good side vision helps protect him from enemies creeping up on him. Remember he has a blind spot directly behind him, so don't walk behind him without giving him notice that you're back there. They don't see as well in the dark as some people think they do."

"My goodness, you certainly know a lot about horses."

"Not really. One of the first things my instructor taught me was about the vision of the horse and to let him, or her, know when I was around. At first I was so nervous I sang all the time to be sure the horse knew it was me.

Now, Dottie, put your hands on either side of his jaws and open your mouth to blow gently in his nostrils. Don't puff and blow; just breath out."

"Why in the world would I do that?"

"Your breath is warm and, hopefully, pleasant. He gets your odor and will remember you."

Jason turned to see an older man grinning at them. He must have been in his seventies. His face was weathered and wrinkled showing a lot of outdoor living and work. His sky blue eyes were keen and showed amusement. He wore jeans, a green flannel shirt, an old dirty-looking hat and boots worn down at the heels.

"Hello. We're here to ride," Jason spoke to him. "I made reservations. I'm Jason and this is Dottie. She has never ridden before, so, I'm hoping this is a well-trained gentle, intelligent horse."

"Y'all just call me Dusty. I been uh working here nigh onto thirty years. Yeah, the horse she's uh standing in front uv is one uv the best. He's twenty-two and has taught loads uh people to ride. He likes people and'll take good ker o her. Lady, you don't need to worry. Poco Bueno will teach you to ride."

"What a relief, Wait! Twenty-two. Isn't that too old for a horse to be working?"

"No, ma'am. I wouldn't run 'im too much or ask 'im to do high jumping, but he's good fer at least six years with good ker, and we do take good ker uv our horses. Sonny, I take it you know how to ride."

"Yes, sir. I learned English when I was a little sprout, but I'm eager to learn Western."

"Lot uh ways they're alike and a lot uh ways they's different. Yore seat and yore body will be the same, but yore hands and yore signals will be different. I'll take you'ns in the training ring and start you'ns out if you like."

"Oh, I'd like," Jason laughed.

"Actually yore legs will be a little different. In English, the stirrup is on the ball of the foot and yore leg is only long enough to let yore knee fit in the front of the saddle. In Western yore stirrup is still on the ball of yore foot, but the leg is longer and more down on the horse's sides."

"Thank you. You can show us as soon as we get mounted."

Jason helped Dottie to mount and checked the saddle to be sure it was secure and she was sitting correctly. He smiled at her. "The kidneys of the horse are right under the saddle, so be sure you don't bang or bump around unnecessarily. I'll lead you into the ring before I mount, then Dusty can tell us how to hold our legs and hands."

Jason took the reins and Poco obediently followed by his right shoulder while his horse, Rampage, followed at his left shoulder. Both horses were beautiful Quarter horses and well trained.

"Y'all go ahead and walk around while I check you'ns out to see how you'ns need to improve--- just for safety's sake," Dusty drawled.

Jaon started Rampage around to his left beside the fence. Poco fell in line and poked along. Dottie held on to the saddle horn for dear life. She hunched over and looked so afraid that Jason was sorry for her when he looked back to check on her. He turned his horse around and guided him to walk beside Dottie.

"There's nothing to be afraid of in here. There's a fence around the entire ring and Dusty and I are both here for you."

"Scuse me, Sonny. Why don't you go on ahead for a while and I'll walk beside the lady and help her."

Jason touched his horse's sides and Rampage walked faster to get ahead of Poco. By then Dusty was walking beside Dottie and could take hold of Poco if he started to walk faster than Dottie was comfortable going.

"Now miss, yore feet are too far in the stirrup. The iron should be on the ball of yore foot. Sit up straight. Now which hand do you write with?"

"I use my right hand for writing," Dottie's voice trembled.

"Then pick up both rains in yore left hand being sure the reins are even on both sides. Hang your right hand down beside you or rest it gently on yore thigh. Now don't that feel better?"

"Why do I let my right hand hang down or rest on my thigh?"

"Sos it'll be free to draw a gun, throw a rope or pick up something. The Western way of riding is for working and that hand needs to be free to work. Now make yore seat muscles tight and gently pull back with the reins."

Dottie followed his orders and was astonished when Poco came to a complete stop.

"See. You control yore horse with the reins and with yore body. If'n you want him to go to the right, lay the reins firmly again the left side uv his neck. Put yore right heel back a tiny bit and gently push the rump away with yore foot."

Dottie did as he directed and gave a gasp of pleasure when Poco turned to the right.

They walked on. "You want him to turn to the left, place the reins agin the right side uv his neck, put yore left heel back a tiny bit and gently push the rump away."

Again Dorrie was thrilled with Poco's response. "That's all there is to it?" she asked.

"Yep. I think you'd better just walk today and get the rhythm of the horse. If'n you come agin, you kin jog. The English call it trot and they do what they call posting by coming up and down in rhythm to the horse's movements."

Dusty instructed her how to pick up the reins and gently touch the horse's side to get him to walk forward. He then walked across the ring to talk to Jason. Actually, Jason was doing well and was turning correctly because he heard Dusty giving instructions to Dottie.

"Dusty, I want more speed, but I'm afraid her horse will follow and she'll fall off and get hurt."

Dusty gave a shrill whistle and a tall, chestnut gelding jumped the fence and trotted to him. Dusty took a hand full of red-gold mane and swung up on the horse bareback. "You go on, Sonny, cross the pasture and I'll stay with yore lady and see to it that she enjoys her ride."

"Is that all right with you, Dottie?"

"Of course. I'm really enjoying this, but I'm not ready for the next step yet."

Jason walked to the gate, leaned over and opened the gate from horseback. He backed his horse out of the slightly opened gate and then leaned over and shut the gate and latched it.

"Hey. You've done that before," Dusty called. "That's good. Now go enjoy yore ride. We'll be fine here."

Jason walked his horse past the farm machinery and went through another gate into the pasture. He talked quietly to his horse often so that the horse would know his voice and be willing to work with him. When he got safely into the pasture, he bumped both heels against the horse's side and Rampage took off. Jason allowed him to go in a run until he was across the pasture. He reasoned that the pasture might be about fifty acres. He didn't want to get out of sight of Dottie, so he guided his horse to run in and out around some trees on the edge of the pasture and then asked the horse to jump a big log laying in the field. Rampage easily jumped the log with his ears up and forward showing that he, too, was enjoying the outing.

In the training ring, Dottie had progressed enough so that Dusty put his horse out of the ring and stepped outside to lean on the fence and watch Dottie.

He called for her to start at one corner and turn her horse to go across the ring to the diagonal corner and then turn the horse to walk around the ring in the opposite direction to what he had been doing.

When Jason returned and dismounted, Dottie was enjoying her horse so much that she didn't want to leave. "I hope we can do this again soon. I saw you out there going like the wind and wanted to do that so much."

"The time will come when you can," Jason assured her. "It's vitally important for a new rider to get acquainted with the basics of riding. It's safe for the rider and the horse. Now your lesson isn't complete. The saddle and bridle must come off and be wiped down and hung up where they belong. Then the horse must be brushed to get the sweat off and make him feel good. Here's a pick. I'm going to show you how to check and clean the hooves."

"All that!" Dottie was amazed. "I thought you just got on and rode and then got off and left. Show me though. I want to learn the right way."

Dusty stood by with a grin on his weathered face because he highly approved of Jason knowing how to care for his mount properly. He finally strolled over and complimented Dottie on how quickly she was learning.

"I heerd my daddy one time tell of his daddy when he lived with his family in a log cabin way off from town. One cold night they wuz sittin around jist enjoying the supper and knowing they were in safe out of the weather. Two men rode up tared, cold and hungry. They asked for food and permission to sleep in the barn overnight. They tied their horses out front."

"When they come in, Papaw said, 'Did you'ns take ker o yore horses?

The men said they would after they eat and got warm. Papaw told them to git out there and take ker o their horse first and then they could eat. They went out, led the horses into the barn and gave them some hay. They took off their tack and gave the horses some water. Only then would Papaw let them in. He said if'n a man didn't take ker uv his mount then he'd be on foot real soon. Sides hit was just right to take ker uv that which was takin ker uv you."

Jason paid Dusty, thanked him and shook his hand. Dottie told Dusty she had truly enjoyed the experience. "Can we come again soon, Jason, please, pretty please?"

"Sure we can. I'm so glad you enjoyed it. I've sure missed working with horse. I've always loved them."

He hooked his arm around the back of her neck and hugged her to his side as they walked on to his car.

# CHAPTER FIFTEEN

April came roaring in with a big wind storm, but no real damage. More people were out working in their yards and Jason felt something stirring inside of him when he observed them.

Taking a walk one day, he went by the barber shop and had to stop and smile. Inside was a tiny boy sitting on a booster seat with a huge cover over him. He was crying and his mother stood by wiping her eyes. *It must be his first haircut. I don't know why, but it's scary for little fellows.*

Jason turned to see a minivan pull to the curb and the driver opened his door to get out. "Hey, Robert." It was Robert Shortt, a photographer from The Blade. "Do you have a camera with you?" Jason called.

"Sure do. Always carry one. Why?" Robert answered puzzled.

"Grab the camera and come here." Robert was soon standing beside Jason.

"See that little boy getting a haircut? I bet it's his first."

"Why is that a shot? Children get first haircuts all of the time."

"Yeah, but that's Major Benjamin Brodi's little boy and Ben's overseas in the thick of battle. He's missing so much watching his son change and grow. I bet your editor would appreciate a picture to send to Ben and include an article in the next paper about what our military heroes are missing at home. Look at those long curls hitting the floor."

Robert rubbed his chin. "Yes, I understand now why you think it would be a good picture and I agree."

Jason smiled and walked on as Robert went charging into the shop.

When he got back to his office, he found a note to call Roger Dawson in real estate. He made the call to the son of Robert Dawson.

"Jason, a place just came on the board this morning and I think it's just what you're looking for. When can I show it to you?"

"How about now?"

"Okay. I'll pick you up in about ten minutes."

Jason hurried out to tell Grace he had some personal business and would be back later. She was curious when Dawson pulled up to the curb and waited for Jason.

They drove down Main for four blocks, then made a left and went to the end of the block. On the left was a red brick with white shutters. There were two bow windows, one on either side of the front. A short porch about forty feet long and about ten feet deep was across the front. A white banister, with curly que trimmings, protected this porch. It would be just right for sitting in a rocker on good nights.

There was a tan, block driveway laid in diamond shapes, leading from the sidewalk to the front door. Jason was pleased to see about fifty feet of front lawn covered with rick-looking Argentina grass.

The front door was an extra wide custom made door with a view of lilies on the glass at the top and four panels of mahogany at the bottom.

Walking through the front door, they stepped on to a marble floor; white with black swirls and about eight feet wide.

To the left was an opening between two eight feet long dividers with custom - made spindles at the top. This was a living room, twenty-seven by twenty. There was the bow window at the front and a four by six window at the side. A fireplace was on the right framed by field stones and a solid oak mantle about eight by two. An opening at the right of the fireplace was a space for storing fuel for a fire. On the left was a wide floor to ceiling book shelf.

Jason was trying to see, in his mind, how furniture could be placed. His mother's valuable Steinway would have a spot in here. They walked back across the foyer to the room across on the right of the front. This was a twenty-seven by fourteen dining room with the bow window at the front and a six by six window at the end. A beautiful French-style chandelier hung from the ceiling. Built in shelves with glass doors were on the left.

After looking out of the two bow windows, Jason was pleased to discover low growing prickly plants that would keep intruders from the windows. They walked to the end of the dining room and through a doorway with a swinging, salon- style door to the kitchen. This room was about twenty-seven by fourteen. There were stainless steel appliances, a large side by side refrigerator and a separate freezer. There were shelves and cabinets that would make any cooks mouth water. The lighting fixtures were all over the ceiling so that there was plenty of light.

At the end of the kitchen was a door connecting with a two car garage.

Going on out into the hallway, there was a half bath at the right at the end of the kitchen.

On past the kitchen area was a twenty-seven by twenty five room bedroom with large walk-in closets lined with cedar wood. There was a full bath and a sliding glass door leading to the outside. A six by four window was at the end behind the garage, but flowering shrubbery and flowers were planted here for a pleasing sight.

At the end of the hall was a door leading to the outside where Jason could see a swimming pool and a gazebo. On the left side of the hall were two large bedroom with large walk-in closets lined with cedar and a full bath between the rooms. There was an enclosed shower and two sinks.

Going out to the back. Jason walked across a ten feet wide tiled flooring to view a forty by thirty pool with rocks and a waterfall at one corner. He could see three feet written at one end going to four, five and finally six feet.

To the left was a white vinyl fence almost covered with four twenty feet tall lilac bushes. Along this side of the house were bulbs of all kinds coming up and some blooming. There were three large trees with a stone bench built circling one of them.

Jason loved the house, but didn't want to appear too eager. He was thinking of putting in a bird bath and more flowers. The gazebo had lattice-work sides and one step to go inside. Benches had been built in around two sides and someone had left padded cushions. There were rose bushes around the gazebo and a rose garden in the rear right corner.

"Well?" Roger beamed as he rocked back and forth from heels to toes.

"What do you think? Isn't this what you had in mind?

Jason turned his back to Roger and pretended to be looking over the yard. "Yes, it's somewhat what I had in mind. What is the asking price?"

Roger told him a reasonable figure that he was surprised to hear, but he kept quiet and started walking to the front beside the house. Anxiously, Roger followed him giving selling points all the way. Finally he was smart enough to stop talking and allow the client to look over the property.

Jason was quiet so long that Roger got antsy. "The owners died and two nieces and a nephew have inherited the property. They want to sell as soon as possible. I think I can talk to them about a better price if you're really interested." Jason was interested but didn't want to appear eager.

"Why don't you talk to them and get back to me," Jason smiled. They got back in Roger's van and went back to Jason's office.

Grace was curious, but was too well-mannered to ask. Jason could see his staff trying hard not to question him. He grinned to himself and finally decided to quit teasing.

Just before closing time, Jason ask them to gather with him in the long room. He told them of going to see the house and what had transpired. They were thrilled for him and wanted to help any way they could.

"I know I'll need some decorating ideas and I'd like to know the name of a good lawnman that I can trust. There will be days that I'll need a good house cleaner, too. We'll talk about that later. Everyone have a good night. See you tomorrow."

* * * * *

Jason, Gary and Nigel were sorry to be bidding goodbye to Tucker. His father had died and his mother was in the hospital with pneumonia. "A family friend called me and told me of the situation. I'm the only one without a family of my own. I'm going to have to go to Arizona and stay with Mom as long as she needs me."

Gary placed a comforting hand on Tucker's shoulder. "You've never said anything about your siblings."

"I have an older brother, Baron, who is married with three children. He is a leading heart specialist and can't get away from Florida to be with Mom. My older sister, Ava, is a teacher married to an attorney. They have three year old twin girls and another baby on the way. I'm third in line and my younger sister has just graduated from college and she and her husband are signed with a church group to go as missionaries. So---" he spread his hands. "You can see why I must go. I'll sure miss you guys. Will you keep in touch and maybe come see me sometime?"

The assured him they would keep in touch and that he would be welcome if he ever decided to return. Steve Nighthawk had been joining them once in a while for bowling, hiking and a variety of activities. Jason, Gary and Nigel started asking him more often until he became one of the group.

One night there were talking in Jason's apartment and Steve was looking as if he had a lot on his mind.

"Steve, you said you were in law enforcement, but you've never told us about your work," Gary urged him to talk.

Steve looked at them with a solemn expression. "My work is why I've been forced to have this R & R. Part of my work took me from Texas into Dayton, Ohio. We wound up all of the case that we could there in Dayton. I had been so emotionally involved that my CO decided I needed a break. A couple of the police in Dayton had been from here and they suggested that I come to relax in a nice, peaceful town with a lot of great people."

"I started as a U. S. Marshall stationed in Texas." He gave a lop-sided smile. "I had always liked the idea of the Texas Rangers, but just didn't seem to make connections. I worked and studied law so that I can eventually get my law degree. Some sleazy scum balls had been operating on the internet to entice children to come to them for illegal purposes."

Here Steve paused to take a long drink of his Diet Coke. "I had a buddy who had been with me in military and now we were together in law enforcement. He and his wife were just like family. They tried so hard to have children with no luck. After a little over four years they were ecstatic to discover they were expecting. They had a little girl and named her Victoria Anne. They ask me to be her godfather. I was happy to do so."

"Their lives were good. It looked as if this was the only child they were going to be able to have. She had just turned fifteen when they began to wonder why she was so secretive and isolated herself in her bedroom so much. She had her own computer and everything that a young woman could want."

He took several deep breaths and put both hands over his face. Finally taking his hands down he continued. The three men understood that what he was telling them was difficult for him to verbalize. It must have been traumatic.

"One morning her father went into her bedroom to get her up for breakfast and school. He found that her bed had not been slept in and she was nowhere to be found. The couple called everyone they could think of, including the school. One girl finally told the principal that he should talk to a girl who had dropped out in her junior year."

"The couple went to this girl's house to talk to her and ask if she knew anything about their daughter. Reluctantly the girl told them that Vicki had met a college freshman on line and had made arrangements to meet him in front of the Star Crest Theater."

"The parents called the police and told them all they had discovered. That's when ICAC stepped in and I begged to be assigned to the case."

"What's ICAC ?" Gary asked.

"Internet crimes against children. There's also the NCAC - national crimes against children. I asked, and was given permission, to work with the ICAC force. After several days of digging, we found other young people who had also been taken in by this internet group; some had not been heard from again and some had returned as if they were shell shocked."

"Weeks went by with very disturbing disappointing happenings. More children disappeared. I had been assigned a young woman as a partner. She was gung ho in her work and doing a fantastic job. She was in her middle twenties but could pass for a teenager. She went on line claiming to be an unhappy fifteen year old who wanted some excitement. She had an e mail from this so called college freshman and made arrangements to meet him in front of the -- surprise of surprises -- the Star Crest Theater."

He paused to drink some water. The men were literally sitting on the edge of their seats. "Four of us had dressed as street people and were hanging out nearby and across the street. She was in bobby socks, oxfords, a poodle skirt and a tight sweater, and her hair pulled back in a blonde ponytail. Her sparkling blue eyes and clear complexion helped her to look much younger than she was. She didn't stand long until a man and woman approached her. They talked and she got in a car with them. We were frightened for her, but what could we do. She was on a job."

"We were afraid for her and thought maybe they had told her they were meeting her for the college freshman. We tried to follow but lost track of the car she was in."

"I didn't tell my friends, but I had learned some horrific facts. These people were not college freshmen, but adults with nefarious plans. They enticed young people and then sold them into sexual slavery or killed them and sold body parts for transplants and a great deal of money. My heart was aching for my goddaughter and all the young people."

"We found they were taking boys and girls, some as young as eight or nine years old, but, for some reason, no older than sixteen."

Nigel broke in with excitement. "Oh, tell us you caught these dirty people and broke up their group. How long did it take you to find all the facts and the gang?"

"We were working for months. They were very clever because they had involved some prominent people in the community. Their reason was money. My partner told us a lot when we finally found her near to death."

Jason was gulping with his anguish and trying not to shed tears. He got up and handed Steve another bottle of water. "If it disturbs you too much to talk about it Steve, we'll understand."

"Yes, it's disturbing, but it's the truth and more people need to know what's going on. As I said we obtained a lot of information from my partner. As far as I'm concerned, she's the hero of this case. She told us that she was appalled to discover a well-known beloved doctor in the community in the gang. He apparently recognized her and they beat her trying to find how much was known about them."

"They finally put handcuffs on her and threw her into a room with a concrete floor. She said there were almost thirty young people in there, boys and girls, one a nine year old girl. Some of the young people had already been used sexually and were beaten badly. None of them had adequate food or water. She overheard the doctor and another man planning on selling her to a Japanese buyer."

"They apparently were concerned after discovering who she was and started to move. They brought in a big trailer, like a horse trailer. The floor was covered in dirty straw. They were all handcuffed to a bar along both sides so that they had to sit and could not be seen from the outside. By the time they arrived at the docks, five of the girls and two boys were dead. They were just taken out and thrown on a trash dump behind a warehouse in a dumpster."

"I'm heartsick hearing about this. I can imagine what families felt. How did you tie up the case?" Gary asked.

"We kept a surveillance on the Star Crest Theater. We had placed another decoy there and arrested the man and woman who came to pick her up. The woman broke first and told us of some locations where they kept the young people and what had happened to them. She alone had a bank balance of over seven hundred thousand dollars for her work with this gang."

"We went to a hotel that she had named and went from room to room finding some youngsters and finally we were ecstatic to find Vicki tied up with electric tape across her mouth on a bed. She was more dead than alive. She was immediately taken to a hospital and treatment began. It took weeks but she slowly came out of it. Needless to say she was emotionally disturbed. She resigned from law enforcement and is working in an office that counsels people and helps them with problems, especially young people."

"But what happened to your goddaughter?" Jason asked worriedly.

Steve placed his head in his heads and his shoulders shook. The three men were silent until he was able to speak again.

"She was one that died. Her parents could not accept reality and finally got a divorce. That upset me because I knew how much they loved each other. I'm hoping they'll get help and come together again."

"I can understand why you needed the R & R," Jason said. "Not only because of the heartache concerning the young people but of your precious goddaughter and your friends. I'm so glad you came to us."

The men joined hands and Jason prayed before they broke up for the night.

# CHAPTER SIXTEEN

Beth became more excited as the day of her wedding drew closer. She babbled about plans all of the time. Her friends first smiled about it, but they began to dodge her or look as if they smelled something bad when she talked on and on.

One day, in the office, she asked Jason to sit and talk to her a few minutes. All four of them sat to talk and were pleased when Franklin happened in.

"Jason, I'm hysterically happy that you're singing. I need to go over some song selections with you. Don't hesitate to say something if you don't agree with me or have a better suggestion."

"Okay. You all heard her. Let's talk about this now."

"Mrs. Kerr has agreed to play the organ and my nephew, Brian, will play the violin. While people are being seated, I would like you to sing "Because He Lives". Do you know that one?"

"Know it and love it."

"The musicians will play a couple of selections. As the groom and the groomsmen come into the room, I'd like you to sing 'When The Stars Go Blue". Then as the bridesmaids and ushers walk down the aisle, I would like you to sing, "Love Me Tender". I know that isn't sung in church, but I'd like it."

"It's your wedding. We'll do, within reason, whatever you like."

"What do you mean, within reason?"

"Well, I refuse to sing in the nude."

They all laughed and Beth blushed, but continued. "As I come down the aisle, I want you to sing, "Isn't She Lovely." As I approach Darrell I want you to sing, "Wind Beneath My Wings". As we light the trinity candle, I would like you to sing, "In The Name Of The Father". As we leave the altar and walk out, I want you to sing, "My Love Is Longer Than Forever"." Are all of those okay?"

"If they're okay with you, I'm satisfied," Jason smiled at her.

"Oh, what a relief. Grace, would you please sit on the side with my parents?"

"What an honor. Yes, of course I'll be part of your family."

"And Greg, you're going to be an usher aren't you, please?"

"Wild horses couldn't drag me away. I would be insulted if you didn't include me."

"Franklin, what can we have you do?"

"I'll sit by Grace and by then we'll have a secret of our own to share with all of you." He smiled and hugged Grace. She ducked her head, smacked her open hand against his chest and went to her desk.

Beth was so excited that she didn't take in what Franklin had said. "While we're dancing after the reception, I want the musicians to play, and if you want to, Jason, sing. You don't have to, but it would be nice. I want them to play, "We've Only Just Begun," "One Boy One Girl" and "Unforgettable". Do you think those are all right?"

"My dear, you will be such a beautiful bride that no one will pay attention to anything else. How are your wedding planners coming along?"

"They have the white satin runner for me to walk on and they're placing big white satin ribbons at the end of each pew with two white flowers crossed on the bow. I'll be carrying a white Bible with Canna lilies and white roses on it. My gown is so beautiful. It's white silk with a V neck puffed shoulders. The sleeves are short but my white gloves will come to the elbow. I can wear white, you know because I'm a v --- oh, well, you know. The gown fits to the waist and the skirt part is full. Rebecca found a diamond-looking tiara with a comb on it to hold my four feet long veil on."

Jason was interested and wanted Beth to be pleased with her wedding, but he didn't know what to say.

She went on. "One of the girls found a wonderful item for me to leave a favor at each plate. It is a beautiful light blue tin box full of mints and on it is written Mint to be together, Darrell and Beth, June 20, 2010.

They have big golden bells with white ribbons on then to hang around the room and a bubble machine to blow bubbles while we dance." She danced around excitedly. Greg smiled, shook his head, and went back to work.

"The groom will be wearing a light blue tux with a gold cummerbund. The groomsmen will be dressed like him. My matron of honor is wearing a light blue gown with gold accessories and carrying a big bouquet of a variety of roses. My bridesmaids will wear pale green with wrist corsages.

The ushers will, of course, wear black tux. Have I left out anything?"

Greg scooted his chair back and grinned at her. "What are you going to feed us?"

"That's easy. The Tasty Tid Bit Caterers are taking care of that." She flounced over and sat down preparing to work.

\* \* \* \* \*

May had a lot of scattered showers. "I know April showers bring May flowers, but what do May showers bring?" Nigel grinned as he shook his umbrella off and left it open inside The Perfect Spouse.

"Mud and spring codes," Annalea Porter said as she hurried by and sneezed. "Excuse me, but I've got a code."

"Oh, you shouldn't be out," Linda Sterling told her as she handed Annalea a box of tissues from a nearby table.

"I had to come. I promised someone a favor," she smiled tightly and hurried off.

Several people had entered at the same time and umbrellas were blooming all over the floor inside the door. Jason and Nigel walked to the front of the room to join Gary, Steve, Curtis and Mark at the refreshment table.

Gary drank deeply of the punch, grinned and wiped his mouth with his sleeve as a kid might do. "I almost didn't come out, but now I'm glad I did."

"Why are you glad?" Mark asked him.

"The gossip. I heard some juicy gossip as soon as I got here."

"For shame," Jason teased him. "You know some gossip and you're not sharing it?"

"Well, you'll be as surprised as I was. It seems that Detective Boggs has not only come often, but he's attracted to Rebecca Glover -- and -- surprise, surprise, she's returning his interest. And, Jason, William Penta has been squiring your old girl, Dorothy Cornett around. Charles Goodman and Linda Sterling are making a twosome and ---"

"Whoa," Jason butted in. "You're sounding like some old granny gossip. I never knew you were so interested in others love affairs and spreading the news."

"Oh, I don't care about their love affairs. All of you know I'm not interested. I just think it's funny. We went for several months with no interest in the opposite sex and now, all of a sudden, couples are springing up like spring flowers," he laughed.

During the evening Jason was surprised at the number of new members. He didn't get to meet all of them, but did remember the names of Cole Berring, Tiffany Trump, Kristi Wheedon, Angelica Ramirez and Alicia Harmon. He left quietly and went on home.

Jason had contacted a good friend of his in Lynchburg and asked him to send his furniture that had been stored. He had left money with his friend with instructions to let him know if more money was needed. The furniture would arrive next week and he knew he'd be busy getting his house organized.

Jason had causally mentioned to his friends that his furniture would be arriving the next Friday afternoon. He was pleased and surprised to find Gary, Nigel, Steve, Greg and Jacob waiting to help any way that they could.

He had previously had the house cleaned and the floors polished. Later he might want to get carpets, but the beautiful wood suited him now.

The men made short work of putting two bedrooms, the dining room and living room together. The kitchen was only partially furnished and the third bedroom would, for the present, be made into an office for him.

He had purchased a barbeque grill. It was set up outside and the men had planned on cooking hamburgers, baked potatoes and Nigel had furnished a salad. There were soft drinks and cake. It was late when everyone left Jason in his new home. He walked around the rooms, loving the house and wishing his mother and grandparents could see what he had done with his life. He felt their loving presence and went to bed thankful for such good friends.

The last week in May, Jason hired a young man named Richard Corwin. Beth was pleased that he came to work in time for her to help train him. She did not work the week before her wedding and planned to not return until after the fourth of July. Richard informed them that he would like to be called Richey and he settled in well.

Grace had asked if she could have the Thursday and Friday off before Beth's wedding on Saturday. Jason thought it had something to do with Beth's wedding and told her they'd get along.

Saturday morning Beth was a wreck. Her nerves were on end. She hadn't seen Darrell but a few minutes alone at the dinner the night before.

His parents had taken everyone to the hotel for a scrumptious meal.

While Beth and her attendants were getting ready, Grace slipped into the back room of the church to speak to them.

Beth ran, half dressed, to hug Grace and thank her for being part of her family.

"Well, my darling girl, you now have an addition to that extended family." Grace held up her left hand and showed a sparkling diamond ring and a wedding band.

"Grace! You got married and didn't let any of us know. You're ours and we would all have loved to be there for you. When? How? What? Who?"

"Jason went with us, at Franklin's request. We went to the courthouse and were married by a judge on Thursday morning. We took a short overnight trip, but will take a longer one later. We felt that at our age, and the fact that we'd both been married, didn't call for a lot of publicity. We're happy."

"Oh, Grace," Beth was shedding tears. "I feel badly that I wasn't there for you. You know how much I love you. Didn't you tell Greg or Richey?"

"No. Only Jason. Now wipe the tears from that lovely face and get to your own delightful wedding. I, or rather we are, so happy for you and pray for the best for you and Darrell."

Grace slipped out while the young women helped Beth repair her makeup and finish dressing. Beth's wedding was beautiful and Jason's voice lent a joy to the occasion. At the reception Beth and Darrell danced the first dance with bubbles floating all about them. Beth danced with Darrell's father while Darrell danced with Beth's mother. Then Beth ran to get Jason and loudly proclaimed, "Folks, this man is not a blood relation, but I love him almost as much as I do my brothers and my father. He's the best boss ever."

The crowd cheered and laughed as they danced jazz.

* * * * *

The days following Beth's wedding seemed almost dull. There was plenty of work for Jason and his crew. He and his buddies attended a few of the get togethers at the Perfect Spouse, but he just didn't enjoy it as he had. He was only happy in his own home.

During the last week of June, Jason decided to have an open house. He asked the Tasty Tid Bits Caterers to prepare refreshments for him. They had delicious finger sandwiches and desserts. A punch was burbling all the time from a fountain pouring into a large bowl.

Jason had invited the neighbors with whom he had become acquainted. His staff, some people from the dating agency and people from church were included.

The neighbor, across the street from him, was a twenty year old widow. Her husband had been killed as soon as he was shipped overseas and he never knew they were expecting their first baby. Eight months after his death she gave birth to a little boy. Jason felt admiration for Roberta Grondin and her determination to make her life worth while for herself and her tiny boy.

His house was crowded with laughing, happy people, some meeting each other for the first time and some greeting old friends. Jason smiled to himself when he looked around at the couples. Monroe Boggs and Rebecca Glover, Dottie Cornett and William Penta, Alicia Harman and Nigel Scovell, Grace and Franklin. He was pleased to see Richard Corwin was paying a lot of attention to Roberta. And he had invited Tony and Betty Dixon to see his new house and meet his friends. *It seems that Gary and I are the only two of our crowd who hasn't found someone. I almost forgot Steve, but he says he is leaving us and won't be living here.*

People were stopping Jason on the street complimenting him on his home and his party. He went out to eat and never ended up alone. Someone was always sitting at his table to talk.

Back in his office, Jason leaned back in his chair and smiled to himself. What a good move he made to the Village of Fayette. It truly was a peaceful village and had lots of great people.

He frowned thinking of Margaret Archer. There were no new developments on her death and Gary had not received any more threatening phone calls.

He slapped his open hand on the top of his desk and opened a folder to start working.

On the last day of June, Jason had a call at home. It was a tearful Greg.

"Jason, mother went peacefully in her sleep last night. I have to be out a few days to take care of personal business."

"I understand, Greg. Please let me know if you need anything or if I can do anything."

"Mother had planned her funeral, but she didn't want a lot of fanfare. She just wanted a few Bible verses, some songs and the usual items that are read about a person."

"Will you need pall-bearers?"

"No. Thank you, Greg, but mother even took care of that. She had it all planned. No flowers. Any donations are to be given to Friendly Arms nursing home for the elderly."

"Greg, I repeat. If you need anything, please don't hesitate to ask. Let us know about the funeral."

"There'll be a viewing tomorrow night and the burial will be the next day."

"I don't expect to see you for at least a week, Greg. Take care, my friend. We will be at the funeral."

# CHAPTER SEVENTEEN

The Village went all out for a fourth of July parade, family picnics in the park, band concerts in the park gazebo and the usual boring political speeches.

The Normal Memorial Library had invited people in to see their renovations and to sign for a library card. Business places had sent flowers and good wishes. Jason sent a potted Elegant Twist Bamboo for the front area and a gorgeous Double Pink Azalea that could be enjoyed inside and then planted out front.

Beth returned on the fifth of July, giddy and full of stories about where they had been and what they had seen. She was busy settling in the home that she and Darrell had bought. Darrell's father had paid the down payment on the house as a wedding present. There was loads of furniture from both sets of parents that had been in the families for years. There was little Beth had to buy for her house. Jason was amazed that she was so thrilled with the antique furniture.

Greg was back and Jason secretly thought he looked more rested and more at ease. The four of them were kept surprisingly busy. Jason began to think he needed to hire an additional person because the work was coming in as if he had wished on a magic ring.

Finally in the first week of August Jason was able to drop in at the Perfect Spouse. There were not many people present. He was delighted to meet a new member, a Greek young woman by the name of Zohra Demopoulos. He joked with her that she was named after Zorro. She said he was very clever, and, she added ducking her head, very handsome.

Jason's crew stayed so busy he remarked that it was almost as bad as being during tax time. He was shocked and pleased. He hadn't been open a full year and was now contemplating hiring a fourth worker.

The last week in August Beth breezed in so thrilled and filled with happiness that all of them thought she might be expecting. "No!" she stated emphatically. "I just wanted to show you what my plans and hard work have done." She held up a college diploma stating that Elizabeth Mitchell Carson had gotten her degree with honors. Jason made arrangements for all of them, Darrell included, to have supper at the hotel one night and celebrate with Beth.

August rolled into September with little temperature changes. The nights were cooler, but flowers were blooming every where one looked and birds of all kinds were winging through the village singing their songs of joy.

\* \* \* \* \*

Steve began to talk again about returning to Texas. His family and co-workers were anxious about him. He had made such close friends that he hated to leave.

One chilly night, Jason, Nigel, Gary and Steve had supper at Jason's house and then decided to take a walk. They were subdued because Steve wasn't really happy about leaving and they hated to see him go. The four young men had formed a close group.

They walked down Main Street and as they passed the alley between the hardware store and the restaurant, Gary caught a movement out of the corner of his eye. He looked into the alley and yelled, "Hey, there." He took off running down the alley with it getting darker as he went into it.

The other three took off after him, but Steve quickly passed him and tackled the man that Gary had seen. The man began to threaten and bluster, but Steve and Gary held on. Jason took in a quick breath thinking he recognized the voice.

"Let me go. You've made a mistake. I've done nothing wrong."

"Then why did you run so fast?" Steve asked.

"Well, if you were in a dark alley and several big men came running at you, wouldn't you try to get away?"

"Maybe, in some cases, but not here in the Village."

By then they had forced the man to the sidewalk and under the light.

"Oh, I can't believe it." Gary exclaimed.

"Holy Catfish," Nigel spluttered.

"Tell me it isn't so. Joseph Harper. What were you doing down there and why did you run?" Jason spoke with authority.

"I told you why I ran. Now take your hands off me or I'll sue every one of you for false arrest and kidnapping."

Steve laughed aloud and held up what he had gone down in the alley to get. He had seen Joe throw something at the dumpster and went back to get it. "Do any of you know what these are?"

Gary, Nigel and Jason looked carefully at the clothes. "These look like Margaret's clothes," Gary almost shouted. "Joe Harper, did you kill her?"

"You can't pin that on me. I will sue young man."

Jason asked everyone to listen. "I think, to be on the safe side, we'd better take him to Chief Mason and notify Detective Snouder. Let them decide what happens next."

Joe Harper began to plead with them to let him go and that they were mistaken. He even shed a few tears begging them not to do anything that would break Elaine's heart.

Chief Mason said, "You should have thought of Elaine before you started your life of crime." He stated when Joe repeated his plea.

"I'm NOT a criminal. Please let me go."

Detective Snouder came struggling in. It was obvious that he had hoped to get to bed early. It was now nine.

"Well, well. What have we here? Give me your story from the beginning, Mr. Harper and make it good. I'm in no mood for frivolity. This is one arrest that has taken me by extreme surprise." Det. Snouder was angry.

Joseph Harper looked around at the men in the interrogation room. A defeated expression crossed his face and he hung his head mumbling.

"Speak up, man. We're not here to hang you or shoot you at sunrise. We're just trying to make sense out of this whole horrid mess."

Joe slowly lifted his head and started talking. "Jason, remember the night that Margaret gave you such a miserable time and the other men told her to get lost?"

Jason nodded but said nothing. He grabbed a straight chair, turned it around and straddled it backward, listening intently.

"Well, Elaine and I talked to her about her behavior. Some of the women had tried to help her and she had just cursed them. We tried to help her, but it was obvious we were wasting our time. I told her if she didn't straighten up we would not renew her membership. She left cursing us and threatening all kinds of reprisals."

"The following day, Elaine and I had finished dinner and I went out to get a breath of fresh air and look at the stars. Margaret didn't even live in our area but she came walking by. I ran out to the sidewalk to try to reason with her again. She lunged at me saying she was going to claim I tried to sexually assault her. She tried to hit me in the face and scratch me. I pushed her away and she fell backward striking her head against the stone wall. It was one of those weird accidents. I panicked when I discovered she had died. I knew it would just kill Elaine."

He looked around but no one said anything. He took a deep breath and continued. "Elaine was in the shower so I called that I was going out for a few minutes. I backed the car out, pulled the body into the back seat and drove around. I was not thinking clearly. Finally I went by the alley and saw the dumpster. I had read about people taking the clothes from someone to keep them from being identified. I know now that was foolish. I took her clothes and threw them back in my car and left her in the dumpster."

"I was so frightened when I went home. I put the clothes in a lawn bag and hid them in the garage. When I went inside, Elaine was in bed reading but very sleepy. I kissed her and she complained about me being so cold from being out in the cold air. I took a hot shower and went to bed. You know what happened after that."

Chief Mason just looked sad. Snouder shook his head and said, "You know if you had called the police that night, you would only have been charged with involuntary manslaughter. You might have gotten off with a year or two and community service. With the people in the agency testifying about Miss Archer's behavior, you might have just gotten community service. When you hid the body, you committed another offense. Now you'll be tried for murder, obstructing justice and goodness knows what all."

Nigel broke in angrily. "Why did you try to kill Alice Daniels? She was an innocent person in this whole mess."

"I wasn't trying to kill her. I got scared when Elaine went into the garage hunting for something. I was afraid she'd find those clothes so I was trying to dispose of them. Alice was walking through the alley and saw me. She started to scream and I was trying to put a hand over her mouth. When Gary came running toward me, I dropped her and, taking the clothes, ran. I was again trying to get rid of the clothes when you saw me this time. It's plain fate. Gary Beaumont both times."

"It was too dark for Alice to recognize me. I didn't know who she was until I heard about it. I'm sincerely sorry but no one will believe me now."

"It's going to be difficult for anyone to believe you. Officer," Chief Mason spoke to a policeman that was in the room. "Detective Snouder, do you want to leave Mr. Harper with me tonight or do you want to take him on to the county?"

"Let's leave him with you for tonight and I'll talk to a judge before you hear from me again. Thank you, gentlemen, for notifying me. My wife doesn't thank you. She says I never get to spend a quiet evening at home any more and that she might as well not have a husband." Snouder gave a sad, twisted smile. "She does understand about my work, but it is hard on any woman to be married to an officer in any branch of the law."

Det. Snouder left and Chief Mason told the officer to place Mr. Harper in a cell by himself.

"What about Elaine?" he spoke loudly. "She'll be so worried. I don't know what time it is. You took my watch and everything."

Jason answered, "It's eleven fifteen. She's probably asleep by now. Do you want us to disturb her now or wait until morning?"

"I don't want her disturbed at all, but if she wakes and can't find me, she'll be frightened."

"I'll send officers, a woman and a man, to tell her where you are. She will probably want to see you, but she'll have to wait until morning now.

I'm sorry for her and sorry for you that you made an unwise decision."

"Be sure your sins will find you out," Jason quoted.

The four young men left and walked back to Jason's. It was not a pleasant evening for them.

"Well, I'm glad now that I didn't leave earlier," Steve commented. "I wasn't here when Miss Archer was found but you told me about it, and, being in law enforcement, I was interested in the case. I'll stick around a little longer. I'd like to be here for the arraignment at least. Good night my friends. How God has blessed me with your friendship."

The men parted and went their way.

# CHAPTER EIGHTEEN

Two days later, Joseph Harper was brought to court for his arraignment. Elaine sat on a bench behind him and sobbed the entire time. Workers and members of The Perfect Spouse were there hoping to be able to say something in his defense.

District Attorney Morgan Crum had been told the entire situation and he was sympathetic, but he had a duty to the public and a job to do. Jason had gotten Attorney Maurice Winston to agree to represent Joe. He knew the story and was sympathetic, but Joseph had tied his own hanging rope when he hid the body and kept quiet.

Bailiff Brodie Markee had entered the court a half an hour earlier. He spoke briefly to the District Attorney and then stood up front and in a commanding voice declared, "Hear ye, hear ye, the court of Fulton County is now open and in session. The Honorable Bascomb Hesburn presiding. All persons having business before the court come to order. This is the case of the state of Ohio and Fulton County verses Joseph Harper. All rise."

Judge Bascomb Hesburn had entered with hurried step and a flurry of his robe. He had pepper and salt hair cut military short. Tall and slender, his hawk-like grey eyes held everyone in obedience. He rapped his gavel once and stated, "Be seated."

"Are all persons connected with this case present and prepared? Are the attorneys for the prosecution present?"

"Assistant District Attorney Jordon Whidden present, your honor."

"Is the attorney for the defense and your witnesses present?"

"Attorney Maurice Winston present your honor."

Judge Hesburn glared at Attorney Whidden. "Present your case counselor."

ADA Whidden stood and stated" "Your honor, Mr. Joseph Harper is charged with the willful murder of Miss Margaret Archer on December 26, 2008. Law enforcement officials have investigated for several months and have now brought this man to justice. He not only took the life of this young woman, but he hid the body and obstructed justice. Our recommendation is that he be incarcerated without possibility of parole."

Judge Hesburn stared at the attorney and then at Joseph Harper. He said, "Counselor, what say ye?" He addressed Maurice Winston.

"Thank you, your honor. It is regrettable that Miss Archer lost her life, however, it was by her own carelessness and not willfully by Mr. Harper."

He proceeded to tell of Margaret's obnoxious behavior at the agency and her stalking of the men. He then told of the confrontation between Joe and Margaret which resulted in her death.

"So you see, your honor, the only crime of Joe Harper's is that he became frightened and his deep love of his wife and his desire to not upset her that he hid the body. He bitterly regrets his actions and is prepared to accept his punishment. He has a home and business in the Village of

Fayette and is a long-time member of the community. There is no danger of his leaving the area without permission. I recommend bail and clemency."

Judge Hesburn half closed his eyes and stared at Joe. "There is indeed enough evidence for a trail. I'm going to set the trial date for January 2010 and ------." He hesitated. "I feel that Mr. Harper acted in poor judgment and is not a hardened criminal. I'm setting the bail at One hundred thousand dollars."

The people in the court erupted in loud cheers and applause. Judge Hesburn rapped his gavel. "Order. Bailiff, clear the courtroom."

Needless to say, Elaine was overjoyed to have her husband back with her. Members of the dating agency were divided. Some, who knew Margaret, felt that Joe should be given community service and forget about it. Others thought he should go to prison.

Jason was upset with some of the comments and really upset at people who tried to drag him into the debate. One day he just said, "Ye who are without sin, cast the first stone." And he walked off leaving a quiet group behind him. He hardly knew what to think.

One night Jason and his friends were at the agency when a siren wailed alerting of a possible fire. Cole Berring immediately ran out leaving his jacket behind. Jason looked bewildered.

Linda Sterling had been beside Cole and she saw Jason's expression. "Cole is a fireman and is a trained, qualified paramedic."

"Good for him. I'm glad to know that." Jason smiled.

He turned to speak to his friends and had to smile to himself. Nigel was busily talking and listening to Alicia Harmon. Then Jason's eyes opened wide with surprise. There were Gary and Angelicia Ramirez acting as if they were a couple.

*Humph. Steve is leaving and all my buddies are interested in someone. That leaves me alone--- again. I don't really mind.*

While Jason was deep in thought, he realized that someone was trying to get his attention. Looking down he saw Lisa Madison smiling at him.

"Hello, Jason. I'm sorry I wasn't able to get to your open house. Everyone is raving about your beautiful home. I'd love to see it some time."

"I'd love for you to visit, Lisa. Why don't you come tomorrow and have lunch with me. I'll be happy to show you around."

Lisa was prompt at eleven forty-five and had brought a bottle of wine. Jason thanked her and sat the bottle down on a kitchen counter. "I hope you like shrimp salad and egg rolls. I also have hot spiced tea."

"I love shrimp and egg rolls, but I don't think I've ever had hot spiced tea.

What in the world is it? Is it like cider?"

"Oh, no. this is a recipe that came down through my family from Scotland. It's actually a lot of fruit and spices mixed with a very strong tea base."

They enjoyed eating and finding out more about each other. After lunch and after he had cleaned the kitchen, Jason took her on a tour of his house and outside.

"There is little left of my blooming shrubbery. I had a beautiful bleeding heart bush that was so full of blossoms, I took a picture of it. The roses were outstanding this year. I've not finished the outside. Next spring I intend to add more. Too, there's a lot yet to do inside."

"I didn't see much to do inside. Everything looks so --- well, special. It all looks like you. Strong but colorful and appealing." She ducked her head and looked embarrassed.

Lisa soon excused herself, thanked Jason and left. He wondered why he was not attracted to her. She was beautiful, intelligent, well-educated and had a wonderful job. *I'm glad she's my friend, but that's as far as I want to go with our contacts. What's wrong with me? Have I just not met the right woman yet or can't I really get over the death of Linda. It's been three years. Is it because she was expecting our first baby? I don't know. Lord, whatever your will for me is, I want to do.*

Curtis Warren and Kristi Wheedon announced their engagement. Elaine and Joe were ecstatic. "This is the reason I wanted a dating agency. So that people could find each other and be as happy as Joe and I have been," Elaine said while leaning her head on Joe's shoulder and placing her arms around his waist.

Detective Monroe Boggs and Rebecca Glover announced that they were planning a Thanksgiving wedding because they had so much to be thankful for. Rebecca asked everyone to call him David. "Monroe David Boggs. His mother named him Monroe after her father and he's always hated it.

Now that his mother is dead, he doesn't feel he'll hurt anyone's feelings. His father is in England and we're unsure whether he can come to the wedding or not. My parents are planning on flying in from Hawaii. Both of my brothers are in military service, so I'm unsure about their attendance."

The next week Detective Snouder came to the office to see Jason again.

"Grace bring us a mug of hot spice tea, please."

Det. Snouder was as perplexed as others had been. He drank the tea and sat back with a satisfied sigh. "This is absolutely delicious. What's in it? May I ask for the recipe? My wife would love this."

"Of course I'll give you the recipe. It came through my family from Scotland, but I'll be glad to share. Now what can I do for you?"

"I'm concerned about Mr. Harper. From what all of you have told me about Miss Archer, it's not a surprise that such a tragedy occurred. There's no need to say I wish he had done differently. It's too late for wishing. I do feel uncomfortable pressing charges against him and wish I could do something to influence the judge to be lenient with him."

"I know what you mean. I, and all of us at the agency, well, almost all, feel that he should not be given a severe sentence. His actions after the fact is what has made it impossible to allow him to get off easily. He acted in poor judgment, and how many of us have made just such poor decisions. He did hide the fact though. I've prayed and agonized over this, but can come to no workable solution," Jason stated.

"We can only hope that a judge will be on the bench during his trial that is kind and understanding. Whomever is on the bench will have to give punishment, but hopefully it won't be too severe. I really came by to tell you how much I've enjoyed knowing you. After this trial, I'm going to retire and take my wife on a long trip. She'll appreciate having a husband after all these years that she's raised the children and stood by me."

Jason jumped up and came around the desk to shake his hand. "I've certainly enjoyed knowing you and learned a lot from your investigation. Thank you for being so diligent and understanding."

Det. Snouder left and Grace came huffing back to Jason's office. "I hope that's the last you'll see of him. He has no business bothering you at your place of business."

"He isn't so bad, Grace, when you get to know him. No, I doubt he'll be returning. In fact, he's making plans to retire."

"Hallelujah!" she grinned and moved hurriedly back to her desk.

Of course the others wanted to know what she was so happy about, so Jason told them of the visit. They were all relieved that Jason was not being involved in anything.

Monroe David and Rebecca came to ask Jason if he would sing at their wedding. "I'll be glad to pay you. I don't want to take advantage of your good nature, or your time," David explained.

"Don't be silly. My singing is a gift from God. I'm happy to share with anyone who wants to put up with me. I'm not a professional singer; I just enjoy it. Let me know what you want to hear."

Rebecca went to Beth. "Okay, girlfriend. Payback. I need help in my wedding now. Jason is going to sing. I'm not going to have the big hoop-de-la that you had, but it will be nice."

Rebecca heard Siobhan singing at the agency and told David she would like to have her sing a solo, and, if Jason was willing, to sing a duet with him. David agreed.

Siobhan was pleased to be included. "My family were all raised Irish Catholic, but I recently joined the Community Church here. If Jason is willing to sing with me, I'd love to."

David had not been raised in church, but he had been attending with Rebecca and was interested in knowing more about it. He had always thought Christians were stiff, unfriendly and no fun to be around. He really liked Jason and admired him. He wanted to be more like Jason.

Jason was delighted to sing with Siobhan. They had a couple of meetings deciding what they would sing. Mrs. Kerr was going to play the organ for before and after the ceremony.

"Rebecca isn't expecting a big occasion. She just wants something quiet, memorable and happy." Jason told Siobhan.

They decided that they would sing "From This Moment" together. Siobhan would sing "All That I Am". Jason would sing "A Living Prayer".

As Rebecca walked down the aisle, they would sing together "Take My Hand" Jason would sing "Beautiful Girl". When the bride and groom were at the altar, they would sing together, "Grow Old With Me." During the lightning of the trinity candle, they would sing together "Great Is Thy Faithfulness".

Beth arranged for the white satin runner for the wedding party to walk on. She had two friends of Rebecca's to help her gather as many beautiful fall leaves as they could find. The best ones would be placed at the end of each pew with a rust -colored bow to hold them in place. A large cornucopia would be on the center of the table with leaves and fruits spilling out of it. Pumpkins and corn stalks would be used for floor decorations at the reception.

Rebecca would wear the traditional white dress of white silk made empire style and a circlet of yellow, rust and red flower buds on her head. She would carry her Grandmother's Bible with a small bouquet of rust and yellow mums. The bridesmaids would carry yellow and cream calla lilies with lily of the valley as a backing. A solid stem would be made of a wire wrapped in white ribbons and a bow for them to hold the flowers.

The bridesmaids would wear rust-colored dresses with a circlet of peach rose buds and rust ribbons on their heads.

Rebecca and David discussed his clothing and he decided not to go with rust-colored tux but to wear the traditional black with white ruffled shirt and string tie.

Jason was pleased for them and glad that David Boggs had settled down and become a fellow to enjoy. They played a round of golf a couple of times and David bowled with Jason, Nigel and Steve one night.

# CHAPTER NINETEEN

There had been a light shower on the first of December which turned to sleet and froze before people could get home from work. Jason was concerned for his staff and asked all of them to call him and let him know they were home safely.

"Jason, my man, what could you do about it if we weren't all right?" Greg teased him.

"If I didn't hear from you, I would know where to start looking and ask the police to check for accidents. I'm not trying to keep you in servitude, just to make sure your safe." he answered Greg.

"I appreciate it," Beth spoke up as peacemaker. She knew Greg did not mean to be sarcastic and didn't want Jason to feel badly.

"I do, too. Thank you," Greg said.

Richard looked worried and Jason asked if he could do anything for him.

"No. Oh, maybe you can. Will you please check with Roberta and see if she and the baby are all right or if they need anything."

"Richey, have you been seeing Roberta?" Jason asked.

He looked embarrassed. "Yes, I have. She's a great gal and has had so much heartache that I'd like to help her have a better life."

Jason clapped him on the shoulder. "Good for you. I'll be delighted to check on her and the baby. Don't ever hesitate to let me know if you need anything. I'm a friend as well as an employer."

"I know and I've been so thankful that I'm with you."

Everyone left carefully walking on the slick surfaces. Franklin walked around and took Grace home in his car. Darrell was waiting for Beth and Greg didn't have far to go.

Jason reminisced about the lovely Thanksgiving wedding of Rebecca and David. *Linda and I had a picture-book wedding. I haven't been able to look at the pictures since her death. Some day I'll get them out and go through them.*

Steve and Jason spent a lot of time together. Jason would smile to himself thinking of how the couples were pairing off. He checked on Elaine often and set his mind at ease that she and Joe were all right.

Joe and Elaine went twice to Maurice Winston's office to discuss his coming trial. Joe was getting more anxious and angry at himself for being so stupid. *If I had just called for help as soon as Margaret fell, we wouldn't be going through this. My precious Elaine is such a trooper. She's holding up better than I thought she could.*

Tucker called Jason to wish him a Merry Christmas and to ask about everyone else. "I'm sorry I'm not there for the Harpers. Basically they're good people. Keep me informed about what's going on?"

"I sure will, Tucker. You're mightily missed, buddy. How is your mother?"

"She's very weak. I don't think she has the will to live after losing my dad. They were high school sweethearts and have been together all these years. That's one reason I was never interested in marriage. I didn't think I could find anyone that would mean the same to me. Maybe some day I'll meet that person. In the meantime, give the Harpers my love and best wishes. Tell Steve I'm glad he's staying. My jaw is dragging the floor hearing about Gary and Angelica and Nigel and Alicia. Haven't you found a lovely lady yet?"

"No, Tucker, and I'm not trying. If it's meant to be, I'll meet someone in the future. The present time isn't appealing. Take care, my friend. Keep in touch."

\* \* \* \* \*

Christmas was very quiet. The weather was bad and the workers and members of the dating agency were thinking of Joe's trial coming up in three weeks.

The snow wasn't as heavy as last year and left quickly, but the air was bitter cold. Everyone was bundled up and only going out when it was necessary.

January, named after Janus, the two-faced god, came in with a rush. Bitter cold winds whipped trees and bushes in a frenzy. Signs were blown down and the road crew were kept busy cleaning up tree limbs off the streets. Traffic lights were swinging alarmingly.

The Saturday before the trial, members poured into the agency to have a last well wishing meeting with the Harpers. Elaine didn't cry, but she went around with moist eyes and tight lips. Joe was friendly but subdued.

"Friends, I hardly know what to say. I don't deserve the loyalty you've shown me, but I'm thankful you've been so caring about Elaine. Please take care of her for me. I can't find words to tell you how sorry I am for this whole mess. Margaret didn't deserve to die like she did and she sure didn't deserve to be placed naked in the dumpster. The only excuse I have is that I panicked and could only think of how heartbroken Elaine would be. It's worse on her now, and I'm sincerely sorry. Thank you for being here and I hope you'll carry on with a lot of love and success." Joe walked out of the room wiping his eyes with Elaine leaning against Rose and crying.

A Sheriff's deputy came to escort Joe to the jail on the night before the trial. He was kept in the holding room of the courthouse until the trial was ready to begin. The bailiff came to escort him to his seat in court.

Bailiff Markee was working this trial. He checked with attorneys from both sides to make sure they had all the supplies and water they needed. He admonished the people crowding the courtroom to remember this was a court of law and they must conduct themselves accordingly.

Finally he stood before the court looking splendid in his blue uniform, even with a pistol on his hip. He stood military straight and proclaimed, "Hear ye, Hear ye the court is now open and in session. The Honorable Judge Martin Sheldon presiding. All present having business before the court come to order. This is the case of the state of Ohio verses Joseph Harper. Would you all rise, please."

Judge Sheldon came in with a smile. His light brown hair was getting thin, but his hazel eyes were sparkling with the joy of life. He was about six feet and a tiny bit overweight. He looked like someone's lovable grandfather.

"Are all persons connected with the case present and prepared? Are the attorneys for the prosecution, and your witnesses, present?"

"District Attorney Morgan Crum for the prosecution, your Honor. We're prepared."

"Is the attorney for the defense, and your witnesses, present?"

"Attorney Maurice Winston for the defense, your Honor. We're prepared."

"Let the record show that all parties in this case are present and prepared."

Judge Sheldon read from a paper in front of him. He looked at Joe Harper as if he would like to say something, but kept quiet.

"Counselor Crum, present your case."

Morgan Crum stood and gave a chilling account of the death of Margaret Archer and of the body being left nude in the dumpster on a freezing night.

He told of the various times Joe was seen and of his "attack" on Alice Daniels.

This took a long time for Attorney Crum to tell of the charges against Joe.

Judge Sheldon listened carefully and took notes. After Crum was seated, the Judge wrote more notes. He then looked at Maurice Winston.

"Counselor, what say ye?"

"Thank you, your Honor." Maurice stood and told of the unpleasant attitude of Margaret's and of the times she was cautioned. He then told of the night of her death and the fact that it wasn't premeditated murder. He then sat down.

He had talked so long that even the Judge took a glass of water. The bailiff had been standing quietly at the left side of the judge in front of the bench.

Judge Sheldon looked at Morgan Crum. "Do you have witnesses?"

"No, your Honor. We feel the facts speak for themselves. Mr. Harper did willfully take the life of a woman and then hid the body and obstructed justice during the investigation." He sat back down.

Judge Sheldon then looked at Maurice. "Counselor, do you have witnesses?"

"Yes, your Honor. We have." He nodded to the bailiff who read from a paper.

"Jason McBride, please take the witness stand."

Jason stood looking very confident in a grey suit with a white shirt and a grey and black stripped tie. He walked tall and sure to the bailiff.

The bailiff held a Bible in his hand. "Place your left hand on the Bible and raise your right hand. Do you swear to tell the truth, the whole truth, and nothing but the truth in this case, under penalty of perjury, so help you God?"

"I do." Jason stated firmly.

"Be seated." Jason took the witness chair.

Maurice stepped in front of him and smiled. "Good morning, Mr. McBride."

"Good morning, Mr. Winston."

"How long have you know the accused Joseph Harper?"

"I've known Mr. Harper a year."

"How well do you know him."

"I've seen him and talked to him at the dating agency that he and his wife own."

"Would you say you've known him long enough to form an opinion of him?"

"I think so. I know he's a good business man and that he is devoted to his wife."

"How well did you know Margaret Archer?"

"Not well at all." Jason proceeded to tell of her calling his office and finally accosting him on the street. He told of the night she made a nuisance of herself."

"Would you say that you could believe Mr. Harper when he tells of her attacking him?"

Attorney Crum jumped up. "Objection. The witness has no knowledge of what Mr. Harper was thinking or believing when Miss Archer was killed."

"Sustained. Careful of the wording of your questions, Counselor."

"Yes, your Honor."

"Mr. McBride, do you have anything you wish to add?"

"Just that it would be a travesty of justice to hold Mr. Harper responsible for Miss Archer's death."

**"Objection, your Honor."**

"Overruled. The witness has a right to voice his opinion as long as he isn't quoting someone else or telling a hearsay statement."

Maurice turned to the prosecutor. "Your witness."

Attorney Crum jumped up looking very pompous. "Mr. McBride," he hesitated and stared at Jason. "Have you had any training in the field of law enforcement?"

"No, I haven't. I'm a CPA."

"Where do you get off telling this court how to judge Mr. Harper?"

Maurice jumped up. "Objection. He's badgering the witness."

"Sustained. Counselor, limit your questioning to facts and to testimony that will give us a broader understanding of the case."

"Yes, your Honor. My apologies."

Mr. Crum kept trying to trip Jason in his testimony and finally saw that Jason was sticking to his facts. "That's all that I want from this witness."

"Counselor, do you have a cross-examination?" the Judge asked Maurice.

"No, your Honor. Thank you."

"The witness may be excused. Call the next witness, bailiff."

Eight more were called all telling about the same thing Jason had. They all told of Margaret's nervous habit of talking too much and too loudly and chasing after the men. When Rose Schilling was asked if she believed Mr. Harper's testimony as to what happened the night Miss Archer was killed, she answered "I was not present to hear or see what happened. I can only believe Mr. Harper and I certainly do."

"Objection!" Attorney Crum said loudly.

"About what?" Judge Sheldon asked him. "The witness was only telling that she can not be a witness to those facts."

Everyone was exhausted. There had been a sixty minute break for lunch and then the trial continued until six. Judge Sheldon looked at the bailiff.

"Bailiff, are there any other witnesses. If so, we'll have to continue tomorrow."

"No, your Honor. The witnesses have completed their statements."

"Does either counselor have further business with the court?"

Both attorney stated that they had completed their work for the day.

Judge Sheldon looked around the courtroom and then at Joe. "The testimony I've heard today is not about a premeditated murder, nor is it about a man with a criminal mind. His actions following the incident demand a punishment according to our laws of this land. I will admit that I need to read the testimonies again and think about this. We'll convene again in two days at nine A.M." He rapped the gavel.

Bailiff Markee stood straight and tall. "All rise." After the judge had left the courtroom, people began to talk and disperse. Joe was led by the bailiff back into the holding room to be taken to his cell later. Elaine was given permission to hug him and talk quietly for a couple of minutes. Rose and Alicia led her out to Rose's car where they could take her home.

# CHAPTER TWENTY

When the court reconvened, there were not as many people present. News photojournalists were in attendance because of the unusual circumstances.

Elaine sat on the front bench behind Joe and was surrounded by members from the agency. She had gotten better control of her emotions and was not sobbing aloud. Every now and then she would wipe her eyes.

Bailiff Markee was in place as he is required to be about half an hour before the court session. He now stood straight and tall with a commanding expression on his face.

"Hear ye, Hear ye, the court is now open and in session. The Honorable Judge Martin Sheldon will be presiding. This is the second day of the case of the state of Ohio verses Mr. Joseph Harper. Would you all rise, please?"

Everyone stood and Judge Sheldon came in looking solemn but not tight-faced. He looked as if he wished he were anywhere but there. He looked over the courtroom and rapped his gavel. "Be seated."

"Attorney Crum, do you have anything you wish to add?"

He stood. "No, your Honor."

"Attorney Winston, do you wish to add anything?"

He stood. "No, your Honor."

Judge Sheldon looked kindly at Joe. "Would the accused please stand?"

Joe stood and Maurice stood by him.

"Mr. Harper, how do you plead -- guilty or not guilty?"

"Your Honor, to be honest I don't know what to plead. It's true that Miss Archer died after I pushed her away from me and she hit her head. I did not plan to have any physical contact with her and was shocked at the outcome. I realize that I did wrong by covering up and, as a result, obstructing justice.

To say I'm deeply sorry for my part in the incident is a weak statement, I know. I am sincerely sorry and am prepared to accept whatever punishment you deem appropriate." he stood with bowed head.

"Mr. Harper, this has been a most unusual case. Because you did not fight, or object, to the charges, a jury trial was not needed. I have the right to decide how this case will end. I know you did not plan on anyone's death, but you did hide the evidence. If you had come forward as soon as you realized she was dead, any judge would have probably put you on probation and community service. Especially with all the testimony from your friends that we heard. However, I must assign punishment as my duty to the public and according to law because of your actions afterward."

He hesitated. "I am giving you five years in prison with time of for good behavior. When you are released, you will serve one hundred hours of community service. May God go with you." He rapped the gavel and stood up.

Bailiff Markee looked perplexed and quickly stood at attention. "All rise." When everyone stood, Judge Sheldon walked out of the courtroom.

The bailiff took Joe back to the holding room, with his attorney and Elaine, to prepare for transfer to a cell. He would be taken to a prison within a day or two.

Elaine was inconsolable. "Oh, Joe, my darling, what will I do without you? No, I must be strong and give you encouragement to do the best you can with your life. I'll always love you and will always be with you," she sobbed.

"Elaine, my love, please get hold of yourself. We have a lot of friends at the agency and at church who will watch over you. The time will pass more quickly than you realize and I **will** get time off for good behavior. You can rest assured, I'll do that. In the meantime I think I'll try to write a book about this experience and hope to advise others to not hide, but be brave and face the truth."

The bailiff took Joe away to a cell and Maurice escorted Elaine back out into the courtroom where ladies were waiting to take her home. They had to clear the courtroom for another trial would start in a half an hour.

\* \* \* \* \*

Jason and Steve were having dinner together at a restaurant. "I have no excuse to stay any longer," Steve laughed. "I wanted to know the outcome of the trial and see how the system worked here."

"I hate to see you go, but I understand. You'll always be welcome to visit any time you wish. I'm sure I'm not the only one who will want to see you before you leave." Jason said with a smile.

"My CO has been after me to return for a medical check-up and my parents and siblings want me to come home. I guess I'll ---" He stopped when Chief Aaron Mason sat down by him.

"Hello boys. I'll apologize for dropping in on you like this, but I felt that I should tell you something in person."

Steve and Jason looked puzzled at each other.

"Steve, I ran an extensive investigation on you and your work. You have an exemplary record. Your CO was more than complimentary about you.

The city council and I have had a couple of meetings and we would like to meet with you, at you convenience, in the next day or two."

"What is this about?" Steve asked haltingly.

"I'm not supposed to tell you, but I will and please don't give me away. When the council talks to you, act as if what they say is a surprise."

"Yes, yes. Go on."

"I'm planning on retiring at the first of April. We have a great group of officers, but the majority of them have very little experience in law enforcement. Too, if I choose someone among the men, there will be hurt feelings. We would like for you to consider the job with your education and experience putting you far ahead of anyone else."

Jason whooped and then ducked his head when people turned to look at them. He grinned and turned his back on the other patrons. "There's a chance for you to stay with us. We would all be tickled pink. I know I would. Your family can come visit you here."

Chief Mason continued, "You will have time to go home and wind up any business you have there. Or, if you decide to not accept the position, we'll have to muddle through. We really need you. Our Village has not had a lot of crime, however, more people are moving in and more people are driving through. We are near some fairly high crime districts. I hope you'll consider this carefully and be prepared to accept. I know I'd retire with an easy mind if you accept. This is my home and I love the place and the people, therefore, I want someone in office who will be as faithful as I have tried to be."

"I need to think about this," Steve said. "I know I should be grateful that I'm considered, but it does come as a complete surprise. I'll be prepared for the meeting with the city fathers," he said with a grin.

"Thank **you**," the Chief answered as he left.

Jason was startled when someone slipped in and sat beside him. He was surprised to see DA Crum. "Hello gentlemen. I'll apologize for sitting down without being invited, but I've been waiting for a chance to speak to you. I waited for the chief to leave."

Jason looked puzzled. "I hope we're not in trouble of any kind. Maybe it's just a guilty conscience, but I can't think of anything I've done---"

"Oh, no," the attorney laughed. "I wanted to say that I was so sorry for Mr. Harper during his trial. I fully understood his situation, but I had an obligation to the taxpayers and to our court system."

Jason reassured him. "We know you have a job to do. I could not respect you if you did less."

Steve interrupted. "One thing has bothered me. There was absolutely no mention of relatives of any shape, form or fashion for Margaret Archer. Wasn't anyone notified?"

"We couldn't find anyone. Surely there's someone somewhere, but they're either too far away, or there's no one close."

"That's shocking. No wonder the poor woman was so determined to find someone. People so alone are so sad." Jason mused.

"Yes, they are, but we don't always know what's in another person's life until it's too late." Attorney Crum wished them a good day and left.

Jason blew a long breath out. "I feel so badly for Margaret, but she didn't have an appealing personality. I guess we, as humans, need to be more thoughtful and kinder to other people."

"No, we can't know what's in everyone's life. We might feel helpless, but we honestly can't do anything about it. Look how my goddaughter sneaked around and got herself killed. No one knew she was even online with what she thought was a college freshman. I wish we could make young people understand that we can't just accept people without knowing more about them. Be kind to people but find out all you can about them before you get involved with them." Steve looked sad.

* * * * *

A few days later Jason went into the office to find an excited Greg. "Hey, Jason. I've found a chance to get a lot of money with little trouble. I just buy into this group and invite others to join and I'll get paid for that."

"Greg! Where have you been? That's a pyramid scam. The only people who make money on something like that are the people at the top of the pyramid."

"What?! Explain, please."

Jason explained how someone started the idea. As people joined they would get the benefit of those people's money. The only way the next layer of people could possibly get any money was to talk others into investing money. They would get a tiny bit, but the major part of the money would go up the pyramid.

"Gee. I never heard of anything like that. What should I do."

"What you shouldn't do is give them any of your money. That's a gamble and a risky one at that. If you want to earn some extra money, study the stock market and invest. It's slower to come to you, but it's much more reliable than a scam. Are you in need of money, Greg?"

"Not really, but I was thinking how mother scrimped and saved and still didn't have enough to pay her medical bills. I don't want that to happen to me."

"Let's hope it'll be many more years before you have to worry about something like that," Jason gently poked a fist at Greg's shoulder.

Going on back to his office, Jason thought of all that had happened in his life. His father's abusive nature, the death of his beloved mother, his grandparents loving him and raising him then their death, the horrible death of his wife and then the problems with Margaret. *Life itself is a gamble. We never know from one day to the next what will happen or if we'll even be here. Grandpa used to say, "Live each day as if you know for sure it'll be your last day on earth."* I guess he meant to trust in God and live the best that we can.

At the next agency meeting, Jason felt good inside looking at the couples who had found each other. He was happy for them. He gave a start of surprise to see Steve and Lisa Madison head to head in a corner alone. *Whoa. Something's going on there. I hope Steve will decide to stay with us and it looks as if Lisa thinks the same. Golly. All of my buddies have found someone and here I stand, as usual, alone.*

Jason gave a start when his thoughts were interrupted by a touch on his arm. He turned to find Siobhan, Linda and Tiffany smiling at him.

"You were looking kind of sad or thoughtful," Siobhan said. "We thought we'd be rude and come to keep you company."

Jason laughed. "I'm not sad. To tell you the truth I was just looking around at my friends who have paired off and I'm happy for them."

"Don't you ever want to get married, Jason?" Linda asked.

He looked at her, pursed his lips and told them briefly about his Linda and what had happened to her. They were upset thinking they had said something to make him remember unpleasant things.

"It's been long enough until I'm accustomed to thinking about it now without breaking down. What have you girls been up to?"

As the evening drew to a close, Jason found himself in a large group of people. He laughed and enjoyed the company, but felt he must get home and prepare for church the next morning. He would be singing a solo, "His Eye Is On The Sparrow". His beautiful baritone would sing it wonderfully well.

Siobhan walked to his side. "I hope to see you in church tomorrow."

"You will. I'm singing a solo."

"Outstanding! I would love to join the choir but I hesitate to invite myself," she laughed.

"Come early and I'll take you in the choir room with me. You have such a lovely soprano that the choir director will be ecstatic to welcome you."

"I'll do that. See ya."

Jason drove home feeling much happier than he did coming from his house.

Siobhan was waiting when Jason arrived for church. He took her into the choir room and introduced her to the director and the choir members. She was warmly welcomed. She thoroughly enjoyed the entire service and assured them that she would return.

Two Sundays later the choir director asked Siobhan and Jason if they would sing a duet the next Sunday. They looked at each other, grinned and agreed to sing. During the week Siobhan went to Jason's house so he could play his piano and they could practice. They decided to sing, "How Great Thou Art."

For a few weeks, Siobhan went to Jason's to practice some of the songs with him. They began to have dinner together a few nights. Jason asked Siobhan to look over his house and give him suggestions for making it look more like a home.

Siobhan loved the house and complimented him on the lovely old furniture he had. She finally said, "I just have one suggestion; you need window dressing."

Jason laughed loud and long. "Hello. Windows don't wear dresses."

"Silly, you know what I mean."

"No, I don't really know, but I can guess. You think I need curtains over the cream-colored vertical blinds."

"Give the man a lollipop. Yes, that's what I mean."

"Well, what do you suggest?"

She walked between the living room and dining room looking and thinking. "Have you given any thought to carpets?"

"No. I like this beautiful wood. It cost me a fortune to get them sanded and waxed properly."

"I love them, too, but think about it. Carpeting would help keep the house cooler in hot weather and warmer in cold weather. Wood is beautiful, but you have to keep it up at least once a year. With carpet you just vacuum and replace it about twenty or more years."

"You're making sense, but I'll have to think about it. Now, back to the curtains."

"I suggest hunter green drapes with a pleated valance and a gold roping. Why don't you go to a store and see what they have displayed and get some ideas."

He looked sheepishly at her. "Would you be willing to go with me some time? I know next to nothing about the subject."

"I would love to go with you. It's time I headed home. Thank you for your hospitality." Siobhan left. Jason watched her back out of his driveway and turn to go home.

# CHAPTER TWENTY-ONE

Steve met with the Chief and the city council. He told them he would like to go home to Texas for two weeks and give them an answer when he returned. Everyone was pleased, sure that he would accept.

Jason drove Steve to the airport. The two men got out of the car and walked into the terminal where Steve bought a ticket and insurance. "I always buy insurance when I travel. Jason, would you keep the policy for me? If anything happens to me you can send it to my parents."

"Sure. I'll be glad to do that for you. This is going to seem like an awful long two weeks to me. I can imagine how your family feels with you being gone for months."

"They knew the department told me to take as long as needed. I hope they'll understand when I tell them of the offer that was made to me. In actuality, I'll be stepping down. My job is a very important government position, but to be Chief of police in a sweet place like the Village will more than make up for it."

Jason placed a hand on Steve's shoulder. "Suppose you change your mind and everyone begs you to stay in Texas?"

"I don't know. I'll face that if I come to it. They're calling for me to board." Steve reached and gave Jason a bear hug. "Thank you, my true friend. I've come to feel very fond of you." He got in a short line and turned to wave when he got to the door leading to the plane.

Jason stayed to watch the plane take off. He smiled at the small children watching through the big floor to ceiling windows as the planes landed and left. They were so excited. His heart gave a wrench. *There was a time when I would have had one of those. How I would have loved it and I know Linda would have been a perfect mother.* He sighed deeply and left to go to his car.

\* \* \* \* \*

Jason didn't try to attend anything at the agency. He had told some of them if Elaine needed anything to let him know. He knew she was being very brave and coming in as often as she ever did.

The second week that Steve was gone he called Jason. "Hey! Good news. I've convinced everyone that I'm not going to be in the back of beyond. My family has agreed to visit with me next fall. My CO wasn't happy but he understood. Chief Mason had called him twice and explained the situation to him. I hope you have some of that delicious spice tea when I get there.

Can you meet my plane?"

"I'll make an effort to do so," Jason teased him. "Of course I'll meet your plane. Let me know the particulars and I'll be there."

"Good. I'll call you in a couple of days and let you know what's what."

Jason hung up with a smile. He was looking forward to Steve's return especially if he was going to work and live in the Village.

The next morning Jason brought his paper in and sat down to breakfast and to read his paper. Bold headline jumped out at him. *Dear God. Not again.* He read carefully about the partially decomposed body of a young woman found on a hiking trail near a river. She had not been sexually assaulted but had been beaten and it sounded as if she had been tortured. She was a twenty year old young woman that had just been hired as a teller at the bank. President Mason Phieffer was offering a reward and Chief Mason was asking for any one who might have seen her with someone.

"Well," Jason said aloud. "They can't blame this on Joe Harper."

The next Friday Jason met Steve's plane and was amazed at himself at how glad he was to see Steve.

"How was your trip and how was everyone? What did your CO say about your job offer? How did your family take it?"

Steve laughed. "Are you going to let me answer one question before you ask another? Let's see. My trip was fine. I was surprised because I didn't realize how much I had missed everyone. My family and everyone are well and happy. Remember I told you about my friends whose marriage broke up when their daughter was killed? Well, they came to their senses and realized they were better off together."

Jason was pleased for them. "I'm so glad they are together again. We all need human comfort and understanding when we have a heartache."

"That's right. Now, how did my CO take it? He was prepared because they had called him two or three times. He knew it was actually a step down but understood that I would like to have the experience. My family was not happy and wanted me to stay in Texas but they agreed to visit me next fall.

Did I answer all your questions?"

"Smarty. Yes, you did. I'm just so glad to have you back. I know we'll both be busy, but it's good to know I can call you and arrange to get together."

"Jason, how is Mrs. Harper? I thought of them so often. I told my CO about it and he felt as I did. Mr. Harper is not a criminal; just a man who made an unwise decision. He'll be out in a couple of years on good behavior."

"Mrs. Harper is a remarkable woman. She rallied more than I thought she would. She had always been so close and dependant on her husband, but she has thrown her shoulders back and took over. I'm proud of her."

Jason took Steve to a grocery store to get some needed supplies before he went home.

"Steve, I would have had dinner ready for you but I wasn't sure if you would want to eat or when. I didn't know whether you had eaten on the plane or not."

"No, they don't serve on most planes now, but my mother, bless her little heart, fed me as if I was being fattened for slaughter. I will only have a cereal and some fruit before I go to bed."

"Come to my house tomorrow night for dinner and I'll have the spice tea you like so much. There'll also be a surprise."

"What kind of a surprise?"

"If I told you, it wouldn't be a surprise. By the way. While you were gone we had unexpected crime committed and it has the county up in arms.

A twenty year old bank teller, Lisa Morrison, was found beaten and dead on one of our hiking trails. She had not been sexually molested but something had been done to her that they're not telling."

"I'm sure sorry to hear about that. No, we don't always tell all the facts to the public hoping that someone will slip up and mention something we've held back. A guilty party is sometimes feeling guilty and will slip up and tell a fact. I know Chief Mason is upset."

"Yes, and so is the sheriff. There was one other case like this just outside of Dayton. As far as I know these are the only two."

"Humm. The person has either just started out or has other killings in other states that we don't know about. Okay. Good night, Jason. Thanks a million, my friend. I'll see you tomorrow night at seven."

Jason went on home, glad that Steve was back and thinking of his own problems. The work in his place of business had picked up so fast that he could not believe it. Tax preparations would start soon and he knew he would be too busy to do any socializing.

The next night Steve be-bopped in full of the joy of living. "I can't believe how glad I am to be back. I need to call the Chief and have a confab with him and maybe the council as well."

"I hope you've decided to take the job and live here." Jason said breathlessly, he was so happy.

"Yes, but don't discuss it with anyone else. I need to talk to them first and let them decide how they'll announce it. Okay, what's that surprise?"

They carried their mugs of hot spice tea and walked into the living room. Jason turned on the lights with a flourish and waited a moment. "Well?"

"Well what? What's the surprise?"

"You're not looking. While you were gone, I attended an estate auction and found a perfectly good Louis XV Savonneries Aubusson. It is the right size I needed for the living room. Of course it isn't new, but it's been cleaned and is in excellent condition."

"I thought you were going to leave your floors bare."

"I meant to but Siobhan thought I needed to rethink that."

"Siobhan, huh. What's been developing in the short time I've been gone?"

"Nothing like you're implying. We sing together in the church choir and she came here a couple of time so we could practice a duet with my piano. I'm glad now I listened to her. Look at the drapes. I got them at the same auction and they blend in with the green designs in the rug."

He had found the hunter green drapes with pleated valance and gold tassels for the living room and dining room. There was a smaller rug under the dining room table.

"Have you done anything else with the other rooms?"

"Not yet, but I'm going to have wall to wall carpeting installed in the bedrooms. I find that getting out of bed on to wood floors is not always a joyful way to start the day, especially if it's cold. I turn my heat down at night and it is sometimes chilly when I first get up."

"I'm with you there man. I like my apartment, but I'd like to find a nice house later. Maybe you can guide me in that."

They sat and talked until it was very late. "I need to go home and you look like you're about to fall asleep on your feet, Jason."

"I've had a few nights that puzzle me. I can go to bed exhausted and lay there wide awake until midnight or after. I tried reading one night and found I could have sat up and read all night. Bad idea."

"Too bad. Maybe you need Siobhan to come sing you a lullaby."

"Get out of here and don't make something out of nothing. See you soon."

\* \* \* \* \*

Jason was asked to be on a committee to plan the October festival for the Village. There would be bands, vendors, fun booths, pie eating contests, cake walks and anything the committee could think of to make it a special weekend.

Jason had asked Steve to pitch in and help while he had some time to do so. Steve thought it was funny to talk in Lakota (Sioux) to Jason and make him guess what was being said.

One day when they were walking in the park, looking at the ground to determine what could be done, Steve touched Jason's shoulder and said, "sunka sapa."

"Okay, I'll bite. What are you saying?"

"Look around you, Jason. What do you see?"

"I see park benches, children's playground equipment, grass, trees, and there goes a black dog trotting across."

"Yes! 'sunka sapa.' Black dog."

"Steve, I'd never be able to wrap my tongue around that pronunciation. It's a beautiful language, but I would think one would have to grow up with it to understand it."

"True. It is easier to learn as a child, but adults can learn also. The one big thing I miss here is my sunkawakan. I may yet get one."

"I hope that isn't some bad disease," Jason replied with a straight face.

"No. It means horse. Sunkawakan sa -- red horse." Steve picked some wild daises growing in the park one at a time. "wanji, nunpa, yamni, topa, zaptan." He handed Jason five flowers because he had just counted one to five.

"That's wonderful, Steve. Why don't you come to my Sunday School class on Sunday and pray in Lakota for the people. They would love it."

Steve looked at him and started: Ate unyanpi, mahptya ekta nanke cin, nicaje wakanlapi kta nitokiconze, hi kta makpiya ekta tokel nitawacin econpi kin, he iyecel. Maka akanl econpi kta anpetu otoiyohi aguyapi kin. Anpetu kin le unqupo, na waunktanipi kin unkakiciktonjapo, unkis tona sicaya ecaunkiconpi kin iyecel awicaunkiciktonjapi na taku wawiyutanyan un kin el unkempt sni po. Tka taku sice cin etanhan eunglaku po. Umna"

"Steve, that was breathtaking. Please tell me what you said."

"I just repeated the Lord's Prayer, or as it's sometimes called, the model prayer. Read your Bible. The Lord didn't say to quote those exact words. What he said was, "Pray in this manner." In other words, Our Father who art in Heaven simply means recognize the power of the Lord and recognize where He is."

"Oh, Steve, please say you'll attend church and share with us. Everyone will welcome you and be sincerely interested."

"I'll think about it. At the present time I need to be making an appointment to talk to the Chief and the council members."

# CHAPTER TWENTY-TWO

"Well, hello Steve. I'm delighted that you decided to return. Do I dare hope that this means you're going to accept our offer?" Chief Mason was glad to hear from him.

"May I come talk to you and the council members? Would Tuesday evening be all right?"

"Excellent. That's our regular meeting night so everyone will be present. They'll be as pleased to hear from you as I am."

On Tuesday evening Steve walked into the council room at seven and greeted those who were present. Chief Mason, Mayor Albert Watkins and six council members, two women and four men, were present. They welcomed him and invited him to sit at the big round table with them.

"Before we get to my news, I'd like to discuss something that concerns me deeply. I heard of the death of the young woman, the bank teller, and the possibility that it might be linked to the one in Dayton. I can't presume to tell the police department how to run their business, but I would appreciate it if you'd allow me to make a suggestion."

"Certainly," Charles Bosley, Chairman of the council spoke.

You have in this community an excellent psychologist with a law degree, an outstanding education and loads of experience. It would be to our advantage to ask Lisa Madison to do a profile on the Unsub (unknown subject) and give our law officials a blueprint, so to speak, for an investigation."

There was a moment of silence and then Claudia Wickins ask, "How much would it cost us?"

"I have no idea. That would be between you and Lisa."

Carol Sizemore looked perplexed. "What do you mean by a profile?"

"A profile tells you something about the subjects life style, possible background, possible motive and whatever the psychologist can determine from the evidence. All of the larger government officials have profilers on the payroll now, such as the FBI. In each case, it has helped solve the crime more quickly."

There was a silence and then Charles Bosley said respectfully, "Let's discuss your personal business and then I'd ask you to leave the room and let us discuss this proposition of yours."

Arnold Parker leaned over the table. "We have been hoping that you will accept the position as Chief of Police. You have a stellar reputation and a great work record. No one can ever replace Chief Mason. There are not enough words in the English language to sing his praises, but we feel that you will come closer than anyone else."

The mayor, quiet until now, said, "Hear, hear."

"Yes, if you'll accept me, I shall be delighted to live and work in the Village. I've made some close friends here and feel that we can work well together. True, the population is increasing and more people are moving in from other areas, or rather they're passing through. I think it's safe to say that criminals would think a peaceful place such as this would be a good place to hide out. Yes, I've observed your Chief and agree that he is the best, but we need to look more to the future and plan ahead so that we're not caught unprepared."

The eight people all applauded. Chief Mason nodded at him. "I see no reason for Steve to leave the room while we discuss a profiler. He can answer any questions that may come up. Besides, if he's going to be working with you, he needs to know how you think and what your plans are."

After a lengthy discussion such as, "We've never done that before" the group finally agreed that they needed to obtain all the help they could get.

Charles Bosley was instructed to contact Miss Madison and ask her to work with them.

Again they welcomed Steve and he left, pleased with the evening.

On Thursday, Lisa called him to thank him for recommending her. She had agreed to work with them pro bono and let them decide whether she would be a permanent employee or not. Steve was excited and happy for her.

On Saturday Steve met Jason and they went to the dating agency. Gary and Nigel were waiting for them. Steve quietly told them of his suggestion to have Lisa do a profile. They were all pleased that she had accepted.

"Keep it to yourselves for a while," Steve cautioned them. We don't want to throw a cog in her work because the wrong person found out what was going on."

After reading the police reports from the Village and from Dayton, Lisa reported to the council on the following Tuesday.

"It is a man, probably a loner with no close friends. He may have dropped out of high school. I strongly feel that he was abused by his parents, maybe an alcoholic, abusive father and a domineering mother. Something is wrong with him. He either has a speech impediment or is a cripple in some way, or has a disfigurement. He feels attracted to the women but feels they are looking down on him or maybe they did reject his advances. I think these killings are new to him, but with his feeling of inferiority, they can accelerate into a series of killings."

Chief Mason sat back and smiled, but all the rest of them were astonished at the profile. There were several questions and then the Mayor turned to the Chief. "Do you think you can take this information and begin to look for someone to fit this description?"

"I sure can. Miss Madison, I can't thank you enough for your input and hopefully we'll consider working with you in the future. Thank you for meeting with us."

Lisa thanked them and left. They continued to discuss the evidence and Lisa's ideas.

A week went by with everyone holding their breath, so to speak, for fear another murder would be committed. Steve had taken a copy of Lisa's profile and had quietly gone to work on his on. He observed everyone coming and going in the Village and even went to outlying areas and looked around.

One day Steve was in a feed store just outside of town when a man shuffled in. He was a good six-three and maybe two hundred fifty pounds. He had shaggy, black hair that needed a cut and certainly a comb. He had dark eyes that were constantly shifting and not meeting anyone else's eyes.

When he discovered Steve looking at him, he hurried out without buying anything.

*Now what was that all about? That doesn't mean he's guilty of anything. It only means that he is unsure of himself with people, or maybe he just came in out of curiosity and didn't intend to buy anything.*

Steve quickly made his way outside but the man had disappeared. He could only have gone into the wooded area back of the store to be out of sight so quickly. Steve drove home with his mind whirling with multiple thoughts.

The next day Steve made arrangements to meet with Chief Mason. He told the Chief of the man. Chief Mason didn't recognize anyone by that description. Steve had thought of something to do. He told the Chief his plan.

They put a notice in the newspaper and over the radio that the bank teller's family had lived too far away to come to the Village. They had her body shipped to them. In the meantime the people in the town, and those with whom she worked, would like to have a memorial service. No flowers. If anyone was interested they could donate to the Indigent Relief Fund.

The service was planned for the following Sunday afternoon in the park. At Steve's suggestion, several officers were in the park with no uniforms. Men and women officers. He had asked Jason to come with him. Jason had been clued in as to what they hoped to achieve. He was not authorized to do any police work, but he could go as a friend to Steve.

There was a surprisingly large crowd in the park. The high school glee club sang some songs and the church youth band played for a while as the people gathered. Even Steve did not know all of the undercover officers wandering in the park.

As the bank president was speaking, Steve looked around and saw the strange looking man trying to stand at the back of the group. It was the same man he had seen at the feed store. Up close Steve could now see that the man limped and had thick, loose lips as someone might that did not have a strong mind.

Steve touched Jason's back and they separated to wander toward the man. They slowly and quietly came up on either side of him. They could see that he was agitated as if he were grieving.

Steve smiled at him. "It's a shame that such a lovely young girl lost her life in such a hideous way."

The man didn't say anything, but he did slant his eyes toward Steve.

Steve spoke gently so as not to frighten him. "Are you sorry that you did this?"

The man dropped his shaggy head and nodded. "Why did you do it?"

He spoke haltingly with a slight stutter. "She was so beautiful and I wanted her for mine. She didn't want me and screamed. I had to shut her up. I didn't want to hurt her, but I had to."

Steve took one arm and Jason took the other. They gently led the shuffling giant over to a policeman that Steve recognized. "This man would like to go with you. He's very sorry that he killed that nice young girl."

The officer was startled and couldn't move for a couple of seconds. He finally took the man's arm and said gently, "Please come with me and I'll give you a ride in my car."

Steve and Jason walked with him while he placed the man in the back of an official car. The officer got a radio out of his pocket and softly announced that he was taking a suspect to the station.

"Steve, I would never have done anything like that if you had not been such a good friend. I was scared spitless. How did you know he would be so easy to handle? He could have gone berserk and pulverized us both. He's big enough."

Steve placed an arm around Jason's shoulder. "I wasn't positive, but according to Lisa's profile he wasn't a dangerous person yet. He was just someone who felt alone and unwanted. That's a chance you take as an officer. I've had partners killed right beside me and bullets zinging all around me, but I've never been as scared as I was this day."

"I would never have known you were frightened. You seemed so in control and in charge of the situation."

The Mayor held a press conference on the steps of City Hall. He gave credit to Lisa for her insights and to the officers for doing a great job. He then surprised the people, and the news reporters, when he asked Steve and Chief Mason to stand by him.

"Friends, I have a sad duty to perform today and a delightful one. Your beloved Chief, Aaron Mason has come to the conclusion that thirty years has been a blessing in his life. He certainly has been in ours. The Chief, city council and I have been searching for a replacement. You read in the papers recently of the great work of one of our citizens. It is my pleasure and privilege to introduce to you your next Chief of police, Steve Nighthawk."

There was a moment of surprised silence and then an eruption of cheering, whistling, applauding and just plain approval. Many of the people had come to know and like Steve. The Mayor had a difficult time getting the attention of the crowd. "And now I give you, Steve Nighthawk"

There was another huge round of approval. Steve smiled and waited patiently.

"Neighbors, friends, I wasn't sure I was the person for this job. I love the work, and as most of you know, I've been a U. S. Marshall in Texas for some time. I now have a law degree, but I didn't want to sit behind a desk. I love the outdoors too much. This is going to be a big change for me. With your help and cooperation, we can make this a town that people will want to move into from all over the world. It has always been a peaceful Village and I've loved being here and knowing all of you. You've heard the poem, "No Man Is An Island". Well, no police chief can do a good job without good officers and good citizens behind them. Thank you all. I know I'll never be able to fill Chief Mason's shoes, and I hope he'll say in the vicinity for a sounding board. Thank you and God bless you all."

Again there was loud applause and people crowding in to speak to Steve personally. He looked over the crowd and finally smiled broadly when he saw Jason and Lisa standing waving to him.

The council was impressed with the profile that Lisa had given them. It was puzzling how she knew so much about the man's character without knowing who he was. They agreed to ask her to give them profiles in emergencies because they didn't feel they could afford to hire her on a permanent basis. There was not that much need for her services. She would be paid for each separate case. That suited Lisa. Her business was slowly picking up. The school board had asked her to talk to them about work with disturbed students. She was happiest when she was needed and working.

# CHAPTER TWENTY-THREE

Joe Harper was not upset because of his incarceration. He knew he deserved it. He was just concerned about Elaine. It made him feel better when friends came to visit and told him how well she was taking charge and doing a great job. He was holding prayer groups twice a week and talking to the prisoners about their future. He hoped they would learn from his, and their own, mistakes, and live a better, more pleasant life.

Jason was so swamped with work he was not able to attend the parties at the agency or visit with anyone. During the second week of March, Steve, Gary, Nigel, Cole and Curtis marched into his office and abducted him to the amusement of his staff. They forced him to go to dinner with them and then bowling. He truly did enjoy himself and admitted that he had missed his friends.

He was still singing in the church choir, and about every other month, would sing a solo. He was content, but was he? Why did he have a hollow feeling inside?

Jason was not surprised when Steve and Lisa announced that they were engaged to be engaged. There were three other weddings within the agency and a couple in the church group. He was pleased for all of them and wished them well.

Toward the end of April Jason took a deposit to the bank. Grace usually took care of this, but he wanted to talk to Mason Phieffer. He blithely walked into the bank, at first not noticing the strange atmosphere, In a couple of seconds he realized something was wrong. He looked to the right to see an elderly man, in a guard's uniform, lying flat on his face on the floor. People in the bank were standing like statues. He stood stock still.

His eyes roamed around and saw the tear-stained face of two of the tellers. Then he fastened on two men who were standing with drawn rifles and shocked expressions on their faces.

One pointed his rifle at a teller. "You told me you had locked that door."

"Y-y-yes sir, I did, or thought I did."

"Hurry up with that money. No telling who else might wander in here. We don't want any trouble."

Jason had to nervously laugh aloud at that. "You're already in trouble. Do you realize what can happen to you. What did you do to that poor old man on the floor? He was too old to have been a threat to you."

"Shut up! No one asked for your lip. That old man's okay. He's just knocked out. Now get over here with these people and raise your hands."

"I wouldn't enjoy doing that," Jason said with a pleasant smile. He had observed two police sneaking up behind the armed men. He wanted to keep their attention on him so the officers could arrest them.

"Well, smart mouth. I don't remember asking you for your approval. Now I want all of you to lie flat on the floor. You people behind that counter come out here and lie down with these folks."

Just at that moment the officers were close enough to touch the men. One of them spoke. "I suggest you follow your own orders. Drop the guns and lie flat on the floor. We have you covered and there's more police surrounding the building."

One of the robbers nervously jerked around and fired his rifle at the same time. Jason felt a sharp stinging in his left side. He put his hand to his side and drew it back covered with blood. He dropped so quickly, someone screamed thinking he was dead. Police came charging in through the front door. There was a lot of shouting. Ambulances were quickly called for Jason and the elderly guard who was only shaken up with a knot on his head.

The newspapers were running front page stories about Jason keeping the robbers' attention until the officers could take them down. He was a hero, but he didn't want to be. It embarrassed him. Steve scolded him and hugged him in relief for his part in the arrest.

There was a chunk out of Jason's side, but no life-threatening injuries. Just his pride. He felt weak from loss of blood and did sleep a lot. One afternoon he opened his eyes to see a blurry vision over him. He blinked his eyes a couple of times to clear them and grinned.

"Siobhan. Good to see you. Did you come to laugh at me for being so silly?"

"Silly, yes. Laugh, no. I was petrified when I heard you had been shot during a bank holdup. What ever possessed you to play Wyatt Earp?"

"Not Wyatt Earp. I didn't even have a gun. And if I'd had one, I wouldn't know what to do with it. I'm leaving that up to Steve and his cohorts."

Siobhan brought him up-to-date on the news of the church and the agency.

"Pastor Charles Black is floating on the clouds and so his sweet wife, Debra. They're thrilled with their first grandchild. A little boy. Everyone is doing well. I'm singing a solo next Sunday. Boy, everyone misses you."

They talked until a nurse came in and wanted privacy to take stats. Siobhan leaned over and kissed his check and left him looking like he had been shot again.

Steve checked on him every day. He was surprised and pleased when Dets. Snouder and Watson came to see him. Another day Rebecca and David Boggs came. Jason was pleased because Monroe David Boggs had turned out to be a nice guy to know after all.

After a week, he was released to go home with strict orders not to lift anything heavy or to lean over until his check-up. Jason hardly knew what to do with all the food that people had brought in. Offers were pouring in daily to clean his house, take care of him and do for him. He appreciated the kindness shown but wanted to yell at people and tell them to let him alone.

He was grateful that Siobhan came every day after school and ran interference for him, especially from the starry-eyed women. She laughed.

"I've always heard that you know for sure who your friends are when you really need someone. Wow! I trip over women every time I come in here."

"I'm thankful for their help and their caring, but I'm not interested in anyone romantically. I wish they'd find someone else to hover over." He didn't see the shuttered look in Siobhan's eyes when she turned away to go into the kitchen.

"I'm truly thankful for a good friend like you, Siobhan. Why can't these other women be like you and let me alone?"

She just smiled and shrugged her shoulders. Siobhan taught special education classes at the local middle school and loved her work. She couldn't have told you why, if you'd asked her, she was taking such good care of Jason.

Steve and Lisa visited often and brought him news of the Village. His staff visited and brought him up-to-date on the work.

"Guys, I don't know what I would do without you. I feel like you're family and I've been so blessed to have you," he told his staff when they came one day after work and brought him a big fruit basket. Richey and Greg had taken turns, and sometimes worked together, to keep his lawn and flowers tended.

A month had gone by before the doctor gave his permission to return to his office. Jason was overjoyed. He stretched and moved and was pleased that he felt no pain or weakness.

The work had seemed to multiply like the proverbial rabbits. Jason realized that he would have to hire another worker. Where would he put everyone?

He sat one afternoon with Grace, Beth, Greg and Richey to discuss who they might hire and what could be done with the space.

Beth stood with her fingers of her right hand holding her chin. "You know, we might be able to make use of this long room by placing two desks together, face to face. We could put the table across the wall beside the refrigerator and everything else could be left as is."

Greg and Richey jumped up to move the long table where they ate or placed papers to work on. They then took two of the desks and placed them face to face in one corner section and placed the other desk in the opposite side with room for a desk to face it.

"Yes." They all agreed at once. "That would work," Richey stated. "We'll have less moving around room because we need the filing cabinets where they are against the back wall."

"Jason, did you ever think you might have to move to a bigger location?" Greg questioned.

"I didn't dream I would get this much business. I'm thankful and so blessed. We'll see."

\* \* \* \* \*

Steve came into the office a few days later to bring him an update on the bank robbers. "We have them in jail here, but much to our surprise, Arizona is asking for them. They grew up in a little town, outside of Flagstaff, called Bellemont. They're first cousins and have a rap sheet as long as your arm. DUIs. B&E, car thieves, and a lot of annoying stuff. They've been in trouble since they were youngsters. Apparently they were passing through and mistakenly thought this was a sleepy little town with poor protection. They got a surprise."

"I'm glad they didn't get what they went in for and I'm glad the elderly guard was not hurt badly. I see they have a younger man on duty now."

"Yes, and the bank manager has asked for us to teach a session on what to do during a robbery and how to avoid a robbery. We're more than happy to provide the training."

"I'm glad that young women had presence of mind to not lock the door when she was instructed to do so."

"She is an old hand at working in banks. She had already set off the silent alarm before they told her to lock the door."

During the next gathering at the dating agency, Jason decided to make a visit. He was warmly welcomed and people crowded around to compliment him and tell him how relieved they were that he came through the ordeal. He enjoyed talking to several people for about half an hour.

He looked across the room and was shocked at himself for the wave of anger and jealousy that swept over him. Siobhan and Fran were standing talking to several young men. Jason didn't recognize most of the men and assumed they were new members. One of them had his arm around Siobhan's neck and pulling her against his side.

*What's wrong with me? It's none of my business what Siobhan does or who she hugs.* He rubbed his chest as if it hurt and became conscience that someone was trying to talk to him.

"Oh, sorry, Charles. I was wool -gathering and didn't see you there. How've you been?"

"I'm jim dandy, Jason. It's you we were all worried about. Boy, you turned out to be a hero. You sure think quickly on your feet."

"Yeah, so they say," he muttered while staring at Siobhan.

Charles Goodman looked over that way. "Is Siobhan someone special to you? We know she went above and beyond to care for you."

"Huh? No, no. I'm sorry, I'm still thinking. I think I'll leave and let everyone have a good time. I've sure enjoyed being back and seeing everybody. Excuse me."

He hurried out and almost ran to his car. He gave himself a good talking to on his way home. *Siobhan means nothing to me. I'm not even interested in a romance. Romance?! I sound like a Victorian novel.*

Siobhan looked around and was disappointed to see that Jason had gone. *Oh, well. I'll see him tomorrow in church. It'll be the first time he's back in the choir since he was shot.*

\* \* \* \* \*

The days tumbled by with work keeping Jason too busy to think about anything else. The following Sunday afternoon, Steve and Lisa came by to visit with him and tell him that they had decided to get married but no time soon.

"I can't tell you how pleased I am for both of you." He laughed. "Steve, remember how we talked about having friends but none of us were interested in a relationship? Well, all of you guys have someone now and I am so happy for all of you."

"Jason, why haven't you been dating Siobhan? She obviously cares about you and I've seen the way you look at her. "

"Oh, no. I like Siobhan and she's been a really good friend, but I only think of her like I would a sister."

There was a strangled gasp behind him. The three of them turned to look at Siobhan standing in the kitchen doorway holding a casserole. She turned and ran back through the dining room and out the front door. In just a few seconds they heard her car start.

Jason was too shocked to move. Lisa looked as if she might cry and Steve looked at Jason as if he too surprised to say anything.

"What was that all about?" Jason finally got out the question.

"**That** was a young woman with hurt feelings. Jason, you dumbhead. She has been here for you every single day. Even in the hospital. Didn't you get an inkling of how she felt about you?" Lisa was angry as only a woman can be when another woman has been hurt.

"No. I just wasn't thinking."

"There! You've hit the nail on the head. You. Don't. Think. What are you going to do about it now? She apparently was bringing you something to eat."

He held out both hands, palm up. "What do you suggest I do?"

Steve placed a hand on Jason's shoulder to make sure he had Jason's attention. "Be honest with yourself. How do you really feel about Siobhan?"

"I don't know," he said slowly. Then it came to him. "Last Saturday, when we were at the agency, I saw a man standing with his arm around Siobhan. I couldn't understand the heated feelings that ran over me like an electrical spark. Anger. Jealousy. I really haven't thought about it."

"It's time you thought." Lisa scolded him. Steve excused themselves and left because he could see Lisa was getting too heated up, and it really wasn't any of their business.

Jason walked through his house, around outside and back in trying to think about what had happened and what he should do. *What would he do if Siobhan never spoke to him again. They had too much in common and she had been a faithful friend. Friend.* He was disgusted with himself. Should he swallow his pride and go to her or let it ride for a few days and hope it would blow over.

*Stupid, Jason. Stupid. You can face an armed bank robber and a giant of a murderer, but you can't face one small woman.*

Gritting his teeth, Jason ran out of the house, locked the door and got in his car. He drove to Siobhan's house, not caring if he was breaking a speed limit or not. He was in front of her house in a matter of minutes. Before his courage failed, he got out of his car and strode to the front door. Ringing the bell he stepped back and then rang the bell again. The door was jerked open.

"Yes? Oh, it's you." Siobhan was too much of a lady to be rude.

"May I come in? I'll get down on hands and knees and crawl in if you want me to."

"Don't be foolish. Come on in." she stepped back and invited him into the living room of her small apartment. He looked through to the small kitchen and saw a casserole sitting on the counter. "Have a seat, Jason."

He sat and took several deep breaths. "Siobhan, I can't tell you how foolish I feel and how sorry I am if I hurt your feelings. I think too much of you and am too grateful for your friendship to hurt you." He waited, but she sat silently and let him stew in his own misery.

"I didn't realize until you ran out how much it hurt me to know I had hurt you. I can't explain my feelings. I have said over and over that I wasn't interested in a romantic relationship and yet the other night, at the agency, I almost came over and decked the guy that had his arm around you."

She gasped but sat still and let him struggle on.

"I guess what I'm trying to say is, while I was denying any feelings for you, deep down they are there. I more than care, Siobhan. I know I would be a lost soul without you. Will you please give me another chance? I'll try my dad level best to be a better man."

Siobhan was laughing and crying at the same time. Jason jumped up and rushed to her pulling her up into his arms.

Her head just fit nicely on his shoulder. She kept her head on his shoulder and cried. He leaned back, placed two fingers under her chin and looked long into her face. Finally he slowly dipped his head and kissed her. She had a double hand full of his shirt and kissed him back.

"Whoa. I didn't expect that. I can't explain my feelings but I felt a tenderness rush through me. I would like to keep my arms around you and hold the world off. I've been alone so long and, for a long time was numb with my loss, that I just didn't realize that I was developing deeper feelings for you. This is a surprise and a shock to me."

"It's not a surprise to me," she said smiling through her tears. "I could see the expression in your eyes when you looked at me, but I just didn't realize that you hadn't recognized it. I knew I felt more than a sisterly feeling for you," she gulped and laughed.

He stood looking at her and then slowly and thoroughly kissed her again. "Am I forgiven? I've been stupid, foolish, careless and anything else you can think of to call me. I'm sincerely sorry. If you'll have me, I want you with my whole heart."

Jason and Siobhan kept their feelings to themselves until after the July fourth celebrations. Other people saw and were happy for them, but said nothing, waiting for the couple to declare themselves publicly.

During August Jason asked Siobhan if she would marry him. He had thought of going to Dayton to a jeweler's but then decided to keep the business in the Village. He remembered that his grandmother had kept her rings for him. One was a gold ring with an oval-shaped jade and diamonds surrounding it. One had belonged to his mother: a Marquis cut diamond on a gold ring.

Jason took both rings to show them to Siobhan. He told her their history.

"If you don't want to accept either one of these, we'll get one for you that you choose. After all, it will be handed down to our oldest child," he grinned.

She laughed at his embarrassed expression. "Oh, Jason, I do want children. I love both of them. Why don't I wear your mother's ring as an engagement ring and your grandmother's ring on the other hand?"

"What pleases you pleases me."

# CHAPTER TWENTY-FOUR

It didn't take long for their friends to see the ring on Siobhan's finger.

Everyone was happy for them. Gary, Nigel and Steve teased Jason unmercifully. "You're the man who wasn't interested in a permanent relationship. Jason just grinned and took it all good naturedly.

Siobhan wanted to get married before school started so they could have a honeymoon trip and get back in time for work. Jason surprised himself when he could understand her reasoning and wanted to comply, although, he timidly suggested they might wait until the next summer. Siobhan looked at him in such a horrified way that he backed down quickly.

The ladies in her Sunday Bible study gave a shower for Siobhan at the church. They had bridal showers in Ireland but nothing like this. She was fascinated and thrilled. She was so pleased that she had been accepted, but she knew everyone was also being nice because they knew and admired Jason.

They played a musical game at the shower. Mrs. Kerr would play the first three or four notes of a song and everyone would write what they thought it was. When she finished with the twenty songs, the person with the most correct answers received a special prize.

Siobhan played a game with them telling something about a famous, or well - known person in the Bible.

Everyone would write the name. The person with the most correct names would win a prize.

There were so many women Siobhan knew she would never remember all of the names. She was grateful for Rebecca keeping a book with names and shower gifts. It would make it easier to write thank-you notes.

Rose, Annalea and Lisa organized a shower for her at the agency. It was unusual to have a shower for a member, but this was a special occasion.

Siobhan was determined and Jason went along with her feeling as if he'd been swept up in a fast carnival ride. She had told some of the young women that in Ireland bells are rung at a wedding because they are considered good luck and prosperity for the couple.

Jason had to go to his office and help his staff. He couldn't just disappear and leave everything up to them. Grace, being motherly toward him, checked on him daily as to whether he was eating properly and if he felt he was being ignored by all the flurry in wedding preparations.

Nigel and Steve came to drag him to an agency party one night. Jason was literally in a fog when he tried to remember or plan. He did overhear some of the women talking.

Zohra, Tiffany and Alicia were getting refreshments and talking. Tiffany looked at Zohra and asked, "Have you found a job yet? I know you must be getting anxious."

"No, I haven't found employment yet. It's getting scary. What's the use of having a college degree if you can't put it to work?"

Jason walked over to them. "Forgive me. I'm not trying to eavesdrop, but I couldn't help but overhear your conversation. Zohra, what kind of a degree do you have?"

"I have a BA in Business Administration and a minor in Accounting."

"Marvelous! Would you consider working for me?"

"Jason, I think I'd love it."

"Come in Monday and meet everyone. If you like, you could work, with pay, for a month and then decide if you'd like to remain with us. May I count on you?"

"You sure may. Jason, I would kiss you, but I know Siobhan would have my head," she answered among the laughter of all of those around.

\* \* \* \* \*

Jason felt as if he'd been picked up in a whirlwind. His friends gave him a bachelor party which he felt he didn't deserve. They gave him several gag gifts, but did give him great gifts for his house. There was a lot of good food and wonderful fellowship.

Dr. Charles Black was delighted to officiate and Mrs. Kerr wiped tears of joy from her eye when she was asked to play the organ. Steve volunteered to play a flute that he had made. It was a Native American flute made of aromatic cedar wood. Jason had heard Steve play and was mesmerized with the beauty of the music.

"My cousin, Benjamin Bear Claw, will be visiting and he plays spiritually on a flute he made of black walnut wood. I'd like to have him play some, also."

Jason and Siobhan were impressed and pleased looking forward to hearing them play during their ceremony. Siobhan was curious about Steve's heritage.

"Did I hear correctly that you're Sioux Indian?"

"That's what people call us. We're actually Lakota. The name, Sioux, was given to my ancestors as a derogatory name by the French. It means little snake. They were called that because they were talented in crawling on their stomachs, through the prairie grass, without ruffling the grass. They could sneak up on the enemy easily in this manner."

Steve delighted Siobhan by softly singing a lullaby for her in the Lakota tongue. She wanted to learn and made him promise to teach her.

\* \* \* \* \*

Zohra arrived early Monday morning and was welcomed by the staff.

Jason had a desk delivered for her and it was placed facing Beth's desk. She did not drink coffee, so brought her Diet Coke in and left it in the refrigerator. She confided to Beth and Grace that her savings was being eaten up quicker than she had planned and she was beginning to panic.

"Jason saved me. I'm so grateful to him and promise to work diligently with all of you. Feel free to correct me at any time. I want to do a good job and help Jason's business any way that I can."

They were impressed with her and immediately accepted her as a staff member. Zohra was only twenty-three, but was mature for her age.

\* \* \* \* \*

The people, who had volunteered to make Jason and Siobhan's wedding memorable, found that their church would not hold everyone who wanted to attend. Gifts were being shipped in from overseas as well as most of the U.S. and Canada.

Mayor Albert Watkins suggested that a reception be held in the park. "Several long tables can be set up and decorated. There are some large pieces of plywood in our storage room that can be laid for a dance floor. Food can be catered or invite people to bring a covered dish, or both. We'll be holding the fall festival in the park next month, so all the equipment will need to be taken out of storage anyway."

There was such a little time that dozens of people helped, running errands, supplying needed items, calling, doing whatever was necessary. Jason was astonished at the people helping plan and do. He had never been someone who would seek the limelight. He was very humble, and this left him with a boggled mind.

Siobhan had her mother send the mother's wedding dress to her. It was fine white silk and lace made Victorian style. It was a tiny bit loose at the top for Siobhan but Marcie Gordon was an excellent seamstress and she volunteered to sew it for Siobhan.

Jason tried to be patient with all the hoop-de-la. He had been married before in a beautiful, formal wedding with a woman he adored, but he knew this was Siobhan's first wedding and he hoped it would be for a lifetime. He just smiled at everyone and continued working with a distracted smile, hoping everything would be pleasing to Siobhan.

Finally the day dawned. It had been impossible for Jason to select one of his friends, at the agency, over the other for a best man, so he asked Greg to fill that spot. He wore the traditional black tux with white pleated shirt and black cummerbund. When he stepped through the side door into the church, he was pleasantly surprised to see the sanctuary so crowded that people were standing up around the side and men were rushing in with folding chairs for them. He felt moist eyes when Steve and Benjamin played some hymns on their flutes and then a Native American song asking the Great Spirit for love and protection on the couple.

He could hardly believe how beautiful the matron of honor was in her cream-colored gown carrying a bouquet of peach roses. The bridesmaids followed in pastel colors carrying baby's breath and day lilies. Finally the organ sounded the notes to welcome the bride. Jason did get tears in his eyes when he saw Siobhan looking like a beautiful Victorian lady. He knew how sad she was that none of her immediate family could attend and he made up his mind to be extra kind and thoughtful to her.

Siobhan had no escort. She came down the aisle proudly and stately. She was beaming with love for him and joy for the occasion. The ceremony was one that would be talked about for years because of the part that both the bride and groom had written their vows. There was hardly a dry eye in the house.

Just before they were to light the trinity candles, Jason wondered why Greg slipped over to the second pew and got in a line with friends. Gary and Angelica, Nigel and Alicia, William and Dottie, David and Rebecca, Cole and Linda and

Mark and Kristi. They all stood and with big smiles ringing a tiny golden bell for about ten seconds. Siobhan was touched that they remembered her statement about the ringing of bells during the wedding ceremony. Jason reached over and, with his thumb, wiped a few tears from her porcelain cheeks.

When Dr. Black introduced the newly weds, everyone stood and cheered. Jason and Siobhan walked back up the aisle with loving wishes being called out to them. Gary took wedding photos while the crowd went to the park.

Jason could hardly believe the crowd. "Half the people in the whole county must be here," he said in wonderment. I can't believe this crowd."

The women had accomplished an amazing day with so little time. A group of men and women had been practicing with their instruments and furnished the music. White satin ribbons with big bows had been strung overhead over the 'dance floor' in an X between trees. Flowering, potted plants had been loaned from a local florist and were placed around the 'dance floor'.

Jason was humbly thankful that they had all made it a special day for Siobhan. *But I haven't lived here that long. While is everyone being so nice? Thank you, Lord, for giving me another chance to have a happy marriage and raise a family.*

The delirious couple toured western states for a trip and stopped in Texas to meet Steve's family.

Siobhan confessed to some of the young women that, when she had helped Jason finish decorating his house, she had hoped to be the one living in it. She was a popular teacher and was too happy to describe her feelings. Jason still felt a little numb because everything had happened so fast.

Jason had only been back at work for a week when he decided he absolutely must look for a larger building. He planned to take Franklin with him unless he and Grace wanted to retire. He would make sure Grace had a good retirement package.

# CHAPTER TWENTY-FIVE

The weekend dawned bright and clear with a temperature in the low seventies for the fall festival. Jason closed his office on Friday and Saturday so his staff could help work and enjoy what was offered. He was thankful it wasn't cold or rainy.

People from all over the county came on Friday because they all knew the children would be swarming in on Saturday. No one minded paying the small fees for various events or food because they knew the money was going for a good cause. Vendors would keep a certain percentage from their booths and the city would get a percentage to be deposited in the benevolent fund for the indigent.

Jason had never served on a committee for such a project. He had been willing to give it his best, but he was overwhelmed when he discovered he, not only was made the chairman, but others on the committee stepped back and let him take over. He begged for their input and some did help.

Jason vetoed carnival rides. "They'll take up too much space and they might be dangerous. We have the swings, see saws, slides and merry-go-round already in the park.

He was, as the old saying is, tickled pink when he got favorable replies from food vendors. There would be a fish and chips rolled in newspapers. The women's sewing club had agreed to take charge of the chicken barbeque booth and also serve a choice of potato salad, macaroni salad or corn on the cob. The men's Saturday Prayer Group took charge of the dogs, burgers and fries. The high school glee club had the booth with all kinds of beverages, both hot and cold. Jason's favorite, funnel cakes, made him prance around like a kid. The volunteer firemen took charge of the booth that had kettle corn and caramel apples. The last food booth was cotton candy. The police patrolled the grounds as long as the festival was open.

The local garden club had the face painting and volunteer members from The Perfect Spouse took charge of the cake walk. Nigel took charge of the three legged races. One for men, one for women, one for boys and one for girls.

The crowd cheered with glee when the five - eight Mayor Watkins paired with his six-two grandson to enter the three-legged race. There was even greater cheering when they won the race simply because they were the only ones who hadn't fallen down.

The Merryweathers loaned twelve ponies, six at a time to work for a short period of time. They didn't want them worn out or maybe hurt. Families brought their own cameras, but Gary had a sign that he would take professional pictures. He had western hats and fake belts with toy pistols.

Children begged to have their pictures made dressed like "real cowboys".

Steve had contacted some nearby Kickapoo Indians who operated a sand painting booth. A person could buy a small jar or a fish bowl. There were containers of all sizes. The native Americans would show them how to make their own sand painting.

Ohio was an Iroquoian word, ohiyo, meaning "it is beautiful".

A farmer had donated about one hundred pumpkins. A person would purchase a pumpkin and was furnished knives and scoops. They would carve a jack-o-lantern. Around three o' clock, three judges would select six pumpkins for prizes. Grace was thrilled when Franklin was awarded one of the prizes.

People from all over the county had donated cakes, some from the bakery and some baked at home. Six TV trays were set up inside a circle with a cake on each one. A person would pay twenty-five cents to march to music around the circle. When the music stopped, the person got to claim the cake beside them. If they had taken a step past the tray, they had to keep walking. The person either beside the tray or would have to take a step to be beside the tray got the cake.

The Boy Scouts, Girl Scouts, 4 -H and Future Farmers of America had volunteered to keep the grounds clean. They had set up big barrels at various places. A couple of the girls made cute signs for the barrels about placing trash in there and keeping their park clean. "Keep your park clean and park your trash here". They were given money for their clubs.

Notice had been sent out for weeks in the newspapers, over the radio and on television about the fall festival in the Village of Fayette. The newspapers took lots of pictures and wrote great articles about the festival.

As the day progressed, Siobhan had to laugh. Every time she came near Jason, she reached up to wipe the powdered sugar from his face and off the front of his shirt. This gave him away that he had sneaked another funnel cake. "It's only for once a year," he kept excusing himself.

The park was open at eight on Friday and Saturday morning and closed both days at eight in the evening. Sunday they opened at two and closed at six.

On Saturday the Princess of Fulton County and her court had been introduced and they rode on a float in a parade down Main Street. Children marched with their pets. Different business had entered a float. The high school band played several patriotic songs as they led the parade behind Mayor Watkins in a convertible and the Chief of Police in an official car.

Jason was glad he had vetoed the dunking booth. It probably would have been too cool to get wet. He patrolled the grounds Sunday evening to make sure the park was left clean.

Monday morning he bounced into work amusing his staff. "As hard as you worked, I'm surprised to even see you here," Grace teased him.

"I could never have done it alone. Too many people worked just as hard if not harder. Boy, am I glad that's over and kick me from one end of the county to the other if I EVER get involved in anything like that again.

# EPILOGUE

The entire group had gathered at The Perfect Spouse out of respect for Elaine. The couples no longer needed dating help, but they had fond memories of the people involved in the agency.

Elaine was touched and ecstatic. "Joe will be so thrilled when he hears how many couples have found each other through our efforts. We have been so very happy together and wanted others to have the same opportunity. Yes, Joe made an unwise decision, but he's writing a book about his dark days in hopes of helping others to not make the same mistake. God bless you all."

With tears in several eyes, Elaine went around hugging everyone and congratulating the couples.

Mayor Watkins and the council members agreed that they made a very wise decision to hire Steve as Chief of Police. He and Lisa would be married near Christmas and they had already found a house not far from Jason.

The couples remained friends throughout the years and shared their good and bad news. They also loved each others children and treated them as extended family.

Fourteen months after they were married, Jason, with his heart in his mouth, rushed Siobhan to the hospital. They, with hearts full of love and thankfulness, were overjoyed to have a strong, healthy little boy.

"Da will be so pleased to know we named the baby after him. James Ian.

I know mum would want me to name him after her father, but we'll have another one," Siobhan laughed happily.

Much to their surprise, and Jason's disgust with himself, they welcomed a sweet baby girl, ten months later. The doctor laughed and said when two babies were born within a year, they called them Irish twins. Three years later they had twin boys.

They agonized over naming the twins. They finally agreed on Michael David and Aiden Piers. Jason was adamant about no more children.

Jason surprised Siobhan by purchasing tickets for her parents to come visit and meet their new grandchildren. Siobhan was tearfully happy.

The Perfect Spouse continued and many more people found the love of their life. Elaine and Joe wish it for you and everyone.

# SOME EXTRA TREATS FROM SIOUX DALLAS

## Spiced Tea

You won't find this recipe anywhere else unless someone got it from me. It came down through my mother's family and was used as medicine by her mother who was a midwife. It was also a beverage that the majority of the people liked and enjoyed it whenever they pleased. It can be sipped any time you please or used for stomach cramps, indigestion, or insomnia.

First make a strong unsweetened tea base. I use ten or twelve Lipton tea bags and enough boiling hot water to have a strong, strong pint when it finished steeping.

To this add a large can of unsweetened grapefruit juice, a large can of unsweetened pineapple juice, and a large can of unsweetened orange juice.

Stir in one full teaspoon of <u>each</u> of the following: powdered cinnamon, ginger, nutmeg, cloves and all spice. The more variety of spices, the better. Stir well together. Add juice from two fresh lemons.

Let simmer until it starts to bubble. Makes one and one half gallons. I store it in the refrigerator and take out a mug as I want it. It will last a surprisingly long time on refrigeration.

It can be drunk as is or sweeten to taste. I do use Splenda most of the time.

## Old Fashioned No Bake Fudge-Oatmeal Cookies

2 cups white sugar
1 cup sweet milk
½ cup butter or margarine
6 full tablespoons cocoa
6 cups dry oatmeal
1 cup peanut butter (I use crunchy)

Cook over low heat stirring often until the mixture is smooth. Remove from heat and stir in 2 teaspoons of vanilla.

Drop on wax paper -- amount determines size of each piece preferred. Allow to cool and enjoy.

## Molasses Taffy

2 cups molasses
1 cup white sugar
¾ cup water
1/8 teaspoon baking soda
4 tablespoon butter or margarine
½ teaspoon vanilla.

Cook the molasses, sugar and water slowly to a hard-ball stage, stirring constantly. Remove from heat and mix in all of the other ingredients. Pour into a greased pan until almost cool. Coat both your hands with butter or margarine. (Takes 2 people) Pull the mixture between the partners and fold it over. Stretch into a long rope and cut into small pieces. Yummy. Enjoy!

# AUTHOR'S NOTE

Dear Readers,

Thank you for choosing my book. You may wonder why I did not describe Jason's wedding as thoroughly as I did others. Jason IS the protagonist (main character) of the story, but the book is primarily about The Perfect Spouse and their plans for other people. Too, Jason didn't want a lot of fanfare because he had a wonderful marriage previously, but he wanted Siobhan to have a memorable wedding day. Why was so much attention given to him? That's called writer's license.

Is there such a thing as a perfect spouse? You tell me. Joseph truly dearly loved his wife of forty years. Elaine meant the world to him. He did not commit a crime maliciously, but the decision he made would inevitably hurt the woman he professed to love. Elaine wanted to name their business The Perfect Spouse because she felt that described Joseph. Did it?

Enjoy this book and be prepared for the next book which I've completed. It's called *Dangerous Hilarity*, but it's geared toward older teens and young adults. I'm working on two adult novels. I'm also doing something new to me. I've started a book on Western / Native American called *Montana Madness*.

Blessings on one and all,
Sioux Dallas

www.ingramcontent.com/pod-product-compliance
Lightning Source LLC
Chambersburg PA
CBHW020833260626
47169CB00003B/961